YOUR BILLIONAIRE'S GIFT

LACEY BUCKLES

ISBN 978-1-913673-28-4

For every reader who took a chance on a new story, a new name, a new spark—thank you for trusting me to lead you somewhere dark, decadent, and just a little dangerous. You made this year unforgettable.

AUTHOR'S NOTE

This book blends romance with elements of suspense and dark temptation. Reader discretion—and indulgence—advised.

As with all *Your Dark Desires* stories, this book is intended for mature audiences only. If high-stakes thriller and explicit elements are not for you, please step away safely. If they are—welcome. This story is written to consume you.

THE BOOKBINDER'S INVITATION

Every gift comes wrapped in mystery, every pleasure shadowed by risk. Some stories whisper of desire; others, of danger. This one promises both.

When power meets temptation, trust becomes the rarest treasure of all. So tell me, dear reader—

Will you uncover the truth... or lose yourself to it?

Come closer, and become *Your Billionaire's Gift.*

CHAPTER ONE

The plastic reindeer blares its song... again.

"Run, run, Rudolph, Santa's gotta make it to town..." Tinny and off-key, the little bastard shrieks every time someone walks past Claire's cubicle. The plastic monstrosity's light-up antlers blink in lurid red and green while half the floor groans under their breath. Claire thinks it's festive. I think it's torture. My eye twitches every time it gets set off. The whole office glitters with tinsel, paper snowflakes hang from the ceiling, and the air is filled with the faint smell of a cinnamon air freshener that someone plugged in down by Accounts.

I don't feel festive. Not this year.

I flick my screen to a boring spreadsheet as footsteps approach. My pulse stutters, a little jolt of guilt—because two seconds ago I wasn't looking at time sheets. I was deep in the guts of Ostoria International's event database, tracing threads I have no business touching. One wrong keystroke and I could've tripped every alarm in the system.

But it isn't IT leaning over my cubicle wall. It's Claire, offering me a brightly-wrapped chocolate treat with a smile.

"Come on, Holly, don't be such a Scrooge. It's nearly Christmas."

I wave her off, force a smile, and keep my mouse steady until she's gone.

A ripple of motion cuts through the office. Conversations stutter, keyboards pause. Senior Management sweep past in a procession of tailored suits and clipped heels, their eyes fixed straight ahead, their perfumes and colognes hanging in the air like privilege. They cut through our cubicle farm like royalty inspecting peasants. Claire's reindeer shrieks again as they pass, belting out that cursed chorus into the tense hush.

Nobody laughs. Nobody dares.

Marcus Blythe leads the procession, of course. VP of Operations. Walking ego with an expense account. He doesn't even glance at us—except maybe to sneer at Claire's decorations, like joy is beneath him. My lip curls. He's everything I hate about this company: pomp without substance, cruelty dressed as competence.

Behind him, the rest of the execs strut by, but the one man who never appears is the one who owns it all. Nicolas Sainz. The phantom at the top of the tower. No photos online. No interviews. No Christmas messages to the staff, not even a head shot in the annual report. Just a faceless name on the highest floor.

He isn't the one I'm watching for, anyway. My interest isn't in the man. It's in the assets.

The ones buried deep in Ostoria's systems. The ones I intend to steal.

I watch the procession file out through the glass doors at the end of the large office before returning to my work. Once I'm certain that there are no eyes on me, double checking over both shoulders, I return to my closed tab and lean in to make sure I'm clicking in the right places, gathering the data I need, slipping just the right secrets into my back pocket. I can't download it here without getting caught. But I have a plan.

Movement tugs my gaze away from the screen again. I click away and close the forbidden VPN tab. It's too risky to continue with this many interruptions. I didn't get this far only to get discovered now. Two years I've been here, carefully working my way into a position to do what needs to be done. Caution should literally be my middle name. It isn't. I don't have one.

"I'm sure you get asked this all the time," Claire says brightly, peering at me over the back of my cubicle again. "But were you born at Christmas?"

I hold back a sigh and look up at her eager and curious face. She has dimples in her cheeks and thick, tight curls of mousy brown hair frame her face.

"I do, yes. Get asked that a lot. But no, I was born in June. A cruel joke on my parents' part."

Claire's face falls. "Really? How sad."

"No, Claire, I'm kidding. My parents just liked the

name. I don't think they realised what a bane it would be. Does any parent deliberately saddle their child with a problematic name?"

She tilts her head and frowns as if giving the question genuine thought.

I roll my eyes and return my attention to my screen. She gets the message and slinks away. But now I'm sat here thinking about my parents. They're the reason I'm here, risking everything like this.

I slide open my desk drawer and lift out the invitation again. I've been looking at it several times a day ever since it appeared on my desk after lunch last week. The paper is smooth and matt black. I run my fingers over the velvet-like card again and a smile tugs at the corner of my lips. The gold foil, serif print is pristine.

Dear Holly Harrington,

You are cordially invited to this year's Executive Christmas Masquerade.

The Langford Room. 21st December, 8pm.

Dress code: Black tie and mask.

A few of my colleagues have been discussing the event over lunch tables and cubicle walls. Few enough for me to realise that not everyone in the company is invited. I'm just a Data Systems Coordinator, one of a hundred people working on the tenth floor. No one special. But I've worked hard and had two promotions since I started working here, so I assume I'm on the radar of someone above me. A handful of other people in my department are going, as well as my line manager.

Excitement isn't the word I'd use to describe my feelings about the invitation. Anticipation is closer. Under other circumstances I might have turned it down, given how I feel about the company I work for. But this is just the opportunity I've been waiting for and it's too good to ignore.

I slip the invitation into my bag, rather than my desk drawer, and glance up at the clock on the wall. 5.25. Nearly time. The buzz in the office mirrors the prickle up my spine. Everyone is waiting for half past and the moment they can switch off their computers and get the hell out of here.

"Are you coming to the pub?" Claire asks brightly over the partition.

"Not tonight. I have plans. But have a good night." I smile broadly in an effort to match her tone even though my insides are churning.

I hit send on the email I've been waiting to deliver, then double check that everything that should be closed on my PC is closed and clear the cache, just as I always do at the end of the day. I scoop up the phone handset on my desk and dial down to the security office behind reception. After two rings, a slightly surly voice answers.

"Security."

"Hi Nige. It's Holly Harrington."

"Oh, hi Holly." His tone shifts completely for me. I hide a smile. "How can I help?"

"I know it's nearly clocking off time, but the request just came through for a guest pass. Can you process it for me now and I'll collect it on my way out? I would be super grateful."

"Of course. I'll do that now. See you in a few minutes."

I hang up the phone just as movement stirs all around me. My colleagues are getting up, switching off their computers, and putting coats on with cheery conversation.

I glance over my shoulder at the frosted glass doors, behind which the senior staff are still in their meeting. Whichever bastard scheduled it for last thing on the Friday before we close for Christmas should probably be taken in for a disciplinary. But it happens to suit me. I grab my bag and set off at a brisk walk towards the doors at the far end of the long room. There are dozens of people filing out from behind their desks and moving the same way as me. I slip past George and Elsie and squeeze past Veronica and Sara, my line manager, who are busy chatting at the end of a row of cubicles. I ignore a few calls of my name, intent upon getting out the door. My dyed red hair swings behind me in its ponytail as my high heels thud on the carpeted floor.

I push open the doors ahead of the rest of the people filing out behind me and am first to the two lifts. I hit the call button and the doors on the right slide open immediately. I step inside and plant a tight smile on my face as people pile in behind me.

I get down to reception along with the mass exodus from the building. Rather than heading out into the brisk London evening, though, I turn right and head behind the reception desks to the door to the security office. I knock and it swings open before I lower my hand. Nigel stands there with my guest pass in his hand.

He grins at me as he hands it over.

"Thanks for this. I owe you one," I say, smiling and batting my lashes. I take the pass and slip it into my leather handbag clutched over my shoulder. My own ID card hangs on a black lanyard around my neck, like most employees in this place. Not the important people, no, they aren't lanyard people.

"Not a problem. Now get out of here, pronto, before someone sucks you back in to do more work."

"Will do, Nige. One more stop first though. Have a great Christmas." I wave and turn away, heading swiftly back to the bank of lifts, adjusting my maroon pencil skirt as I go, acutely aware of Nigel's gaze on my backside. Hey, you use what you need to use to get what you want, right?

The lifts empty of their passengers and I brace myself against the tide of people rushing past me. I get back into the empty lift, tap my own security card against the reader at the top of the panel and push the button for the tenth floor. I grip the strap on my bag in a slightly clammy palm and take a deep breath. I can do this.

The doors slide open with a ding and I almost bump into Claire as she steps into the lift.

"Oh!" She startles and presses a hand to her chest. "I thought you'd gone."

"Forgot my coat," I reply, tapping my temple like a ditzy girl.

"Oops, you'll need that in this weather."

We circle each other, her stepping into the lift and

me out of it.

"Certainly will. Good night, Claire. Have a good Christmas."

"You too."

The lift doors close and I drop the smile and jog to the doors into my office. I stride along the walkway, the wall to my left and the rows of cubicles to my right. A few stragglers remain but it's almost empty. The frosted doors to the conference room are shut but I can make out dark shapes through the glass. The meeting hasn't quite finished. I slow my pace, not wanting to get my timing wrong.

Just as I pass the small kitchen, the conference room doors open and people in suits spill out. Claire's ridiculous reindeer sets off as I pass her desk and I fight to retain control of my face as the management team moves towards me.

I keep right as they file past me and quickly duck into my row. I scurry to my desk and scoop up my coat from the back of my chair. I glance over my shoulder just as Marcus Blythe steps out of the room, laughing loudly at something the man with him said.

I pop open an extra button on my black shirt, turn in a flurry and collide with the VP. A soft *whoosh* escapes my lips. His hands clutch my upper arms.

"Woah there," he says, still half laughing.

"I'm so sorry, sir," I say, glancing up at him through thick lashes. One hand rests on his firm chest, the other lightly lands on his ID card where it hangs on his belt. The clip catches and doesn't come away. I press myself more firmly against him and lightly wet my lips.

"It's Holly, isn't it?" he asks, still firmly gripping my arms.

"Yes, that's right." The clip comes away and I conceal my relief. I palm the card and extract myself from his grip, folding my coat over my arm to hide the card fully.

"Working late?" He glances past me at the rapidly emptying office.

"I just forgot my coat," I reply, lifting my arm slightly. "I have to get going. I have to get ready for tonight." I bat my lashes at him again.

"Tonight?" His gaze dips to my cleavage. He isn't even subtle about it.

"The Masquerade, sir."

"Oh. You're coming to that?" He leans back a touch and quickly scans my body.

"I am." I give my head a slight shake so that my long ponytail bounces behind me.

"Well, perhaps you can make up for bumping into me with a dance."

"Perhaps. But how will we recognise one another? We'll be wearing masks." I give him my most flirtatious smile.

"Oh, I don't think that'll be a problem." His smile doesn't reach his eyes. I fight a grimace as he reaches for me and runs the back of his index finger down my upper arm.

"Well, I'd better go." I turn and walk away from him. My heart hammers and my palms are greasy. I clutch the ID card in my hand under my coat. His footsteps pick up speed and he draws level with me.

"I'll walk you out," he says, placing his hand on the small of my back.

I take a deep breath and glance up at him. Even in my three inch heels I'm significantly shorter than him. He's broad too, filling out his dark grey suit. It's a shame he's such a slime ball, because otherwise he'd be just my type. Who am I kidding? My history is full of slime balls.

Claire's cubicle is coming up. Two meters, one... I know what's about to happen. The wretched thing lights up and starts to bleat its tuneless song. I knock it with my bag and it tumbles to the floor, one antler breaks and the music whimpers to a halt.

"Oops," I say, glancing up at him.

A grin spreads across his face.

I hate that I did it. But I want him to want me. When we resume walking, his hand slides down from my back to the curve of my arse.

We reach the lifts and a few of his management colleagues are waiting for one to arrive.

"Are you bringing a date, this evening?" he asks, his lips a little too close to my ear.

I shake my head, manoeuvring myself slightly away from his wandering hands. "Nope. I'll be all alone."

"Then maybe we'll have more than one dance."

"Maybe." I grin up at him, masking my revulsion. "If you play your cards right."

He clucks his tongue just as the lift doors open with a *ding*.

I follow the others into the lift, leaving Marcus behind. I cast him a questioning look and he tucks his hands into his pockets.

"Alas, I'm not done. I'm going up." He glances towards the ceiling. The private offices of senior management are all on the twelfth floor.

"Right. See you later then," I say as the doors slide shut. I almost breathe a sigh of relief before remembering that the lift is full of his colleagues who most likely caught parts of that whole exchange. I keep my gaze fixed on the doors as the lift descends and ignore the whispers at my back.

In the lobby, I carefully tuck Marcus's ID into my bag and put my coat on. Nigel is behind the desk and gives me a nod as I pass.

I follow the flow of people out into the biting cold and pull my black coat tight around me. I fish in my bag for my second phone, the burner that no one knows about. I tap out a quick message:

All set.

I hit send to the only number in the contacts.

Good work. The reply flashes up on the screen. *We'll be watching tonight. —D*

Something unpleasant churns around in my gut.

That was the easy part. Tonight will be the real challenge.

CHAPTER TWO

The lift doors glide open on the twelfth floor and my breath catches in my throat.

This isn't an office space—it's a glittering dream perched over London. The wall along the right side is nothing but glass, stretching floor to ceiling, the city spread out beneath us in a million points of light. Fairy lights drape in golden arcs across the beams, and a Christmas tree taller than the lobby downstairs commands the centre of the room, its branches heavy with glass baubles and strands of red velvet ribbon.

The air shivers with music—strings and piano, weaving familiar carols into something lush and sinuous. "Carol of the Bells" drifts over the hum of voices, all champagne laughter and the low murmur of masked men in tailored tuxedos.

I pause just inside the doorway, suddenly too aware of my own skin. The green velvet of my dress clings to every curve, scandalously low across my chest, flowing to the floor and slit high on my thigh. The gold sequinned clutch in my hand feels absurdly small compared to the weight of what it carries: my phone, my burner, one credit card, and two passes I shouldn't have. My mask matches the dress, dark green and edged in red and gold sequins, a spray of green feathers fanning out to contrast against my red hair.

My fingers dance over the gold pendant against my chest. Sleek, shiny, and concealing a secret. I quickly release it and grip my clutch in both hands instead.

I should feel glamorous. Instead, I feel like an imposter.

Women in gowns that sweep the floor glide past me, glittering like jewels in candlelight. Men in sharp tuxedos and Venetian masks cluster in groups, the air thick with the perfume of money and ambition. Their champagne flutes sparkle in the light of the chandelier overhead, and when they laugh, it's the sound of people who have never worried about rent or debt or their parents' house.

I force myself to step forward. One, two, three strides. The slit of my dress parts with each step, flashing just enough leg to keep the eyes on me that I want, and to make me feel exposed to the ones I don't.

A waiter materialises at my elbow with a tray of champagne. I take a glass, if only to keep my hands busy, the cold glass stem steadying me. The bubbles fizz against my lips—bright red, deliberately bold, like armour.

I tell myself this is just another system to infiltrate,

another network to navigate. I've spent two years playing the quiet girl at the desk, the diligent analyst no one bothers to look at twice. Tonight, I'm visible. Tonight, I'm a mask, a dress, a glass of champagne in hand.

And tonight, if all goes to plan, I'll walk out of here with far more than a hangover.

A hand closes lightly on my arm and I almost spill the champagne.

"Holly!" Sara's voice cuts through the din, warm and steady as always. My line manager looks every inch the consummate professional, even in a floor-length gown the colour of midnight, her mask glittering with discreet crystals. Her blonde bob is perfectly smoothed, her lipstick neat and understated, her posture as polished as her quarterly reports. She's in her forties, confident, self-assured. Professional even when wrapped in satin.

"There you are. I thought you might try to hide in a corner."

"Me?" I force a laugh. "Never."

She gives me the kind of look that says she knows better and tucks her arm through mine, guiding me towards a small knot of colleagues.

"Everyone, this is Holly from Systems. Holly, you remember Andrew, Patrick, and Philip?"

Two men from Compliance, one from Marketing. Masks or no, they look exactly like they do in the office: self-satisfied smiles, expensive watches, too much aftershave.

I shake hands, exchange polite hellos. One of them —Patrick, I think—grins. "Systems? You're the ones who keep us all out of trouble, right?"

"Something like that."

"Careful," Andrew cuts in, chuckling. "That's the department that knows everyone's dirty secrets."

They all laugh. I smile like I'm in on the joke and take another sip of champagne.

Sara saves me. "Don't let them tease you. Holly's the one who makes sure the rest of us can actually do our jobs. Half of you wouldn't be able to find your own expense reports without her."

The men laugh again, but this time with an edge of agreement.

"So," Philip says, lowering his glass in the direction of another group across the room. "Speaking of expense reports... look who finally shows his face."

I follow his gaze before I can stop myself.

A circle of executives stands just beyond the Christmas tree, voices low, body language taut with attention. At the centre is a man I don't need an introduction to.

Nicolas Sainz.

Even masked, there's no mistaking him. Broad shoulders in a tuxedo cut sharper than glass. Dark hair pushed carelessly back, catching the glow of the chandelier. A matte black mask trimmed with gold frames half his face, leaving his mouth exposed—the strong line of his jaw, the faint curl at the corner of his lips.

He isn't speaking. He doesn't need to. The others lean in, watching for his reaction, adjusting their laughter to his cues.

"He looks taller in person," Andrew murmurs.

Sara clinks her glass gently against mine, her smile amused. "Don't look so stricken. He won't bite."

I almost choke on my sip of champagne. "I wasn't —"

"Yes, you were." She tilts her head, studying me like she does quarterly spreadsheets. "You've never seen him before, have you?"

"Not in person." I try to sound casual, but my voice comes out softer than I intend.

"That's because he rarely ventures below this floor." Sara lowers her voice, conspiratorial. "Half the company only believes he exists because the payroll clears. I wonder what his net worth is?"

"Nearly eight billion pounds," I say, carelessly revealing my interest. Yet he's still a ghost on the company website. Invisible unless he wants to be seen.

Sara's eyes widen as she turns to me.

The men chuckle, one of them whistles, but my gaze is still clinging to our elusive CEO. On the way his fingers move slowly over the stem of his glass, deliberate, unhurried. On the way his head lifts just slightly, as though he's listening to something no one else can hear.

And then—God help me—his gaze sweeps the room. Searching, assessing. For a heartbeat, it snags on me.

Heat prickles over my skin beneath the velvet. He

doesn't pause long, not enough for anyone else to notice, but I feel the weight of it. Like he's stripped the mask away already, laid me bare among the glittering crowd.

Then he lowers his glass, murmurs something to the man beside him, and the crowd shifts, swallowing our CEO in tuxedos and sequins.

I exhale slowly. Too slowly. My hand trembles against the stem of my glass.

Everyone else is already turning back to their conversations, laughter swelling again, but I can't shake the feeling that the room has shifted.

That I've been seen.

Sara turns back to the others, launching into a story about last year's masquerade and how half of Finance ended up at karaoke until three a.m. The men laugh, filling in the blanks with their own drunken memories.

I laugh too, though I wasn't there. My attention is caught on the faint vibration in my clutch.

I lower my glass, pulse ticking hard in my throat, and edge a step back from the group. "Excuse me," I murmur. Nobody notices.

My fingers slip into the sequins and close around the burner phone. The screen lights up with a single message.

Enjoying the view? Don't forget why you're here.

—D.

I glance up, throat dry. The room is full of masks and sequins, everyone glittering, everyone laughing. Any one of them could be watching me.

I slip the phone back into my clutch before Sara notices my hand shaking. She glances over her shoulder, smile bright. "You all right, Holly?"

"Fine." My voice comes out too fast. Too thin. I clear my throat. "Just... fine."

She studies me for a beat, then lets it go, turning back to the men.

But I can't shake it. The sense of eyes on me. From Nicolas. From the people I really work for. From every angle at once.

CHAPTER THREE

The champagne fizzes sharp in my stomach, nerves coiling tighter with every tick of the clock. I circle the edge of the ballroom, eyes darting between exits, stairwells, the doors marked Private. Looking for a crack, a moment to slip through unnoticed.

Not yet. Too many eyes. Too much laughter.

I keep moving, mask slipping into a polite smile for anyone who meets my gaze. Sara is across the room in animated conversation with the CFO, her hands carving arcs in the air as she tells some story. My colleagues are already tipsy, clustered near the bar. I should be safe. Invisible.

Then a hand clamps around my wrist.

"Miss Harrington."

Marcus Blythe.

My heart lurches as I turn. He looms in front of me, his grey mask a mockery of Roman marble, his grin smug enough to curdle milk. His tux is perfectly cut, of course. His cologne hits like a wall.

"Sir." I pitch my voice light, deferential.

"You owe me a dance," he says, already tugging me towards the dance floor.

I let out a nervous laugh. "Do I?"

"Don't play coy." His hand settles at the small of my back, too low, too firm. "You promised earlier, remember? After our little... collision."

Heat creeps up my neck. Not the good kind.

I could protest, but that would draw attention. And I can't afford eyes on me tonight. So I paste on a smile and let him lead me into the throng of dancers.

The band slides into something slow and sinuous, strings wrapping around us as Marcus pulls me closer than necessary. His palm presses against my spine, his other hand enclosing mine like a man staking claim.

"You clean up well," he murmurs, his breath warm against my ear. "Systems isn't usually this glamorous."

I laugh again, brittle. "Flattery doesn't suit you."

He chuckles. "It's not flattery if it's true." His gaze dips brazenly to the neckline of my dress. "I could get used to seeing you like this."

My stomach twists. Every instinct screams to step back, to break free. But I keep the smile, keep the mask. One wrong move could unravel everything.

Across the floor, laughter ripples from another circle of dancers. I risk a glance, and there—Nicolas Sainz, watching. Masked, unreadable.

For a heartbeat, I swear his gaze lingers on me.

My pulse stutters.

Marcus tightens his grip, forcing me back into step. "Eyes on me, sweetheart," he says softly. "You don't want to make me jealous."

My gaze flicks back, but Nicolas has already turned away, swallowed by the crowd.

I grit my teeth behind my smile and let him guide me through the steps. His grip is too tight, his movements more about ownership than rhythm.

"I was disappointed not to ride in the lift with you earlier," Marcus says, leaning in as if sharing a secret. His breath smells faintly of whiskey.

"Bad timing, that's all," I say lightly, though my pulse betrays me.

He smirks. "I'd hate to think I scared you off." His thumb strokes lazily against my spine, a territorial gesture that makes my skin crawl.

I focus on my breathing. In. Out. Just another system to navigate. *Play along until you can step away,* I tell myself.

Marcus leans closer still, lips brushing the shell of my ear. "Strangest thing happened this afternoon. Could've sworn my ID card was attached to my belt during that tedious meeting but when I came back upstairs—poof. Gone."

My throat tightens. So does my grip on my sequinned clutch, pressed precariously between my left hand and Marcus's shoulder.

I keep my smile fixed, though my pulse drums in my ears. "Maybe you dropped it?"

"That's what I thought." His chuckle vibrates against me. "But I'd hate to think someone took it. That would be... unwise."

He pulls me closer, pelvis pressing against mine as the strings swell.

Every instinct screams to shove him back. Instead, I tip my head, laugh like it's a joke, and whisper, "Who would dare?"

Marcus studies me, eyes sharp behind the mask, like he's testing for a crack. Then his grin returns, wolfish. "You're right. Who indeed?"

The music shifts, the tempo quickens, and I seize the moment to spin out of his grasp. My skirt flares, the sequins of my mask catching the light. I twirl back into his arms just as the crowd erupts in laughter around us, but the reprieve is fleeting—his hand slides lower again, to the curve of my hip.

"Careful," I murmur, forcing a playful lilt. "You'll crease the velvet."

He laughs, delighted, as though I've given him permission. His hand slides possessively against my hip. My skin prickles—not with attraction, but with the desperate need to escape.

The song ends. Applause breaks out. I step back quickly, dip my head in a quick bow, and retreat before Marcus can tighten his grip again.

"Don't go far, Holly," he calls after me, voice rich with promise. "We're not finished."

I keep my smile plastered on until I'm swallowed by the crowd. My hand clamps around my clutch, nails digging into the sequins as though the thin shell of fabric and glitter can guard the secrets inside.

Weaving through the sparkling crowd, my pulse is still skittering from Marcus's slimy hands on my body. The applause fades, replaced by another swell of strings, but I barely hear it. I fix my gaze on my mark—a client with a reputation for drinking too much and saying the wrong thing at these events.

I slip away from the crush of bodies toward the row of lacquered doors marked "Ladies", slipping the guest pass out of my clutch and concealing it in my palm as I follow her. The music muffles behind the wood, and the bustle thins to the close sound of heels and perfume. My pulse is a tiny drum under my ribs.

She stumbles over to the basin—an older woman in a silk sheath, perfume rich enough to make my head swim. Her hair is swept up, earrings like tiny moons. She leans close to the mirror to inspect her make up, leaving her purse and mask unattended on the polished marble beside the sink. She catches my eye in the mirror and a smile spreads across her face.

"Fabulous party again, isn't it?"

"It's Vivienne, right?" I ask, leaning against the counter in front of her belongings.

"That's right." A slight frown creases her botoxed brow.

"We met at the spring gala."

"Oh, of course!" She returns to her own reflection. She doesn't recognise me. We've never really met, but she's too tipsy and too polite to say anything.

While she's focused on herself and chattering about the canapés, I slip her guest pass out of her purse and replace it with the one I had Nigel make earlier.

"You know?" I interrupt her rambling and offer her a conspiratorial smile. "They've opened a private tasting in the function room at the far end of the ballroom," I tell her. "If you ask for the rosé with the gold flecks, they'll seat you. Very exclusive, but your pass should get you past the doors." The lie tastes metallic on my tongue, but she drinks it like a cocktail.

"Oh. I'll have to check that out. Thanks!"

"So lovely to see you again," I say. I slip into the furthest cubicle and wait for her to leave. I slip back out, snap her pass in two and drop it into the bin. Following her out, I spot her making for the door to the function room.

I skirt the crowd and pause by the door into the corridor that leads to the executive suites. I lean around a group of suits to see Vivienne trying her keycard at the door, a red light blinking with each frustrated swipe.

The door beside me bursts open and a security guard strides towards Vivienne. I slip through the door unnoticed and it swings shut behind me, muffling the music into a distant hum.

The corridor is hushed, lined with dark wood and frosted glass. A stairwell curls upwards, leading to the mezzanine that overlooks the ballroom. I climb quickly, heels clicking, nerves ticking louder than the music below.

At the top, I pause. Through the railing to my left I can see the chandelier blazing over the party, the swirl of gowns and masks, Marcus already prowling towards another unsuspecting partner. Sara's head tilts back in laughter, her pearls flashing. All of it looks impossibly far away, like a stage I've just stepped off.

Up here, the air is different. Colder. More dangerous. The corridor stretches ahead, leading towards the executive suites. The carpet here is thicker than downstairs, the wood more polished. And the smell, not the cheap, chemical crap served as "ambience" that we have on tenth. This corridor smells of luxury.

I check over my shoulder. No one followed. My clutch is heavier now. The pendant hums against my sternum like a heartbeat. I pass offices for all of the senior management on my right, their names etched into brass plaques beside each door. I approach the door at the end and reach into my clutch for Marcus's keycard.

One light tap on the pad beside the door and the light turns green. I slip through the door and rest against it, closing my eyes for just a moment while I take a breath.

I'm in.

CHAPTER FOUR

Two doors stand opposite one another to my left and right. To my left is an impressive set of double doors leading to Nicolas Sainz's office. But I turn right. A brass plaque glints in the low light: *Vice President of Operations: Marcus Blythe.*

One tap against the reader, and the lock clicks green. I slip in through the door and the motion-activated lights flicker to life.

The office smells of cedar polish and Marcus's overpowering cologne, clinging to the leather chairs. The lights are low, soft amber, the sources concealed so just their warm glow is visible against the walls. A dim lamp also stands on the desk. Papers in neat piles held in place by a tacky paper weight, a single tumbler with a slick of amber liquid at the bottom, his ego stamped on every detail.

I shut the door behind me and cross to the desk, my

heels muffled by the thick carpet. My clutch thumps onto the polished surface and Marcus's keycard skitters across it as I slide into his chair. The leather groans under me, a sound too loud in the hush.

"Okay," I whisper, to no one but myself.

The monitor wakes with a tap of the keyboard, the login prompt glowing. My heart rattles against my ribs. I know the code. Numbers matched to his birthday, his arrogance making him predictable.

The desktop blooms with icons. My breath quickens.

I move quickly, navigating the folders I mapped in stolen minutes back at my workstation. Compliance, Discretionary Clients, Executive Files. There it is—CLIENT_DISCRETIONARY_HALCYON_2025.enc. The name alone is a confession.

I lift the pendant from my throat and click the hidden catch. The gold bar slides apart, revealing the USB tip gleaming like a secret tooth. My hands tremble as I slot it into the port. A folder opens, ready.

The progress bar crawls across the screen. Too slow. My fingers drum against the desk, against the clutch, against my own thigh. The hush presses closer. Every second feels like a shout.

I glance toward the door. The corridor is silent. The music from below a faint, muffled thrum.

Halfway.

I scoop up my clutch and squeeze it against my chest, the sequins biting into my skin like tiny warnings.

Come on, come on, come on.

The progress bar crawls like molasses. Seventy percent. Seventy-one. My pulse is so loud I almost don't hear the faint vibration in my clutch.

I snatch it open. The burner phone glows.

Update. Now. —D

My throat tightens. My thumbs itch to reply, but the copy isn't finished. If I stall, he'll know. If I answer, I'll lose seconds I don't have.

I shove the phone back into my clutch and grip the desk edge hard enough for my nails to bite.

Eighty percent. Eighty-two.

The hush presses close, heavier than silence. The faint hum of the ballroom below is almost gone up here. I'm alone. Too alone.

Then—footsteps.

Two sets, echoing down the corridor. One steady, one uneven, the rhythm slightly off. My blood freezes.

Eighty-seven. Eighty-eight.

The footsteps stop just outside. Voices.

Marcus. Slurred, lazy. "I'm telling you, Nick, someone's been in my files. You know how it is—staff think they're clever, poking their noses where they don't belong."

Nicolas. Quiet, sharp. "What member of staff would risk it, Marcus? You leave your card lying about, you invite trouble."

Ninety-five. Ninety-six.

Panic claws up my throat. The bar will never reach a hundred before they walk in.

The handle rattles.

One hundred.

I yank the USB free, slam the pendant closed around my neck. My fingers fly across the keyboard—control, lock. The screen goes black just as the reader beeps and the door clicks.

No time. No thought. I drop to the floor and fold myself into the dark beneath the desk, clutch crushed between my chest and my knees, my back pressing against wood.

The door opens. Light shifts across the carpet.

Marcus stumbles inside, his cologne hitting me like a blow. Papers rustle, glass clinks.

"Ah. Right where I left it." The sound of plastic against wood—his access card scooped up from the desk where *I* left it seconds ago.

My stomach flips.

Nicolas doesn't move. I can feel his stillness, the weight of his presence, as if the air is different with him in it.

Then his voice, low and venomous. "You need to stop, Marcus."

A pause.

"What?" Marcus laughs, too loud. "Stop what?"

"You know what," Nicolas hisses. "The way you touch them. The way you look at them. It won't be tolerated."

My chest squeezes so tight I almost choke. My fingernails bite into sequins, sharp points digging into my palm. He doesn't say my name, but every nerve in my body screams he means me.

Marcus scoffs. "It's harmless. They like the attention."

"Do not mistake fear for interest," Nicolas snaps. The sudden steel in his tone makes my heart stutter. "One more complaint, and you'll answer to me."

The room stills. Marcus mutters something unintelligible, a sulky shuffle of shoes on carpet.

Nicolas inhales slowly, then exhales, a sound like a blade being sheathed. "Go back downstairs. Smile. Dance. Leave the staff alone."

The door clicks closed. Footsteps retreat.

For a long moment, silence floods the room again. My heart hammers hard enough to shake my ribs. My pendant digs into my sternum. I press my forehead to my knees and whisper a prayer I don't believe in.

I'm still alive.

For now.

My burner phone buzzes again.

I take it out with shaking hands.

Were you careful? Report. —Daryl

I'd like to think he cares about my well being. But I know better.

I was. Job done. Just waiting for my exit.

I wait until the silence is thick enough to choke on, until I'm sure the footsteps have faded down the corridor. My knees protest as I unfold from under the desk. I grab my clutch, check the pendant is cool and shut against my skin, and force myself upright.

One last look at the black screen, at Marcus's neat desk—a fountain pen next to the keyboard; a small stack of papers weighted down by a gaudy, bronze bull; and an empty in-tray. No trace left behind. No proof.

I slip out into the corridor, closing the door with a whisper of sound. My legs feel like water. My heels thump too loud against the thick carpet, each step a drumbeat. I hurry down the curved staircase and into the last stretch of corridor.

Halfway back to the door that leads into the ballroom, it swings open.

My heart jolts.

A security guard steps through, broad shoulders filling the doorway. His radio crackles softly at his hip. His eyes fix on me at once.

"Evening, miss," he says, tone professional but edged with suspicion.

My mind races. One second. Two. Then I let my knees loosen, my shoulders dip. I plaster on a tipsy smile.

"There you are," I say, voice breathy with feigned relief. "I've been looking for you. Someone said there was a private tasting... with the pink wine? The one with the little gold bits floating in it? I have to try it." I widen my eyes and sway just enough to sell it.

His frown deepens, but the suspicion thins. He sighs, shifting his stance. "You shouldn't be back here, miss. These corridors are restricted."

I giggle, pressing a hand to my lips. "Oops."

He rubs his jaw, mutters something under his

breath, then gestures firmly to the open door behind him. "Come on. Back to the ballroom."

"Yes, sir." I give him a mock salute, wobbling slightly on my heels as if the champagne's got the better of me. My insides are still ice, but my mask is bright and foolish.

He escorts me through the heavy door and into the swell of music and light. My pulse thuds like it's trying to break free.

I can feel his eyes on me as I walk away. So I keep the act going, smile plastered on, swaying toward the bar with a lazy flourish. Leaning against the bar with a champagne flute in hand, staring right at me, is Nicolas Sainz. Shit. I have to keep up this act with his eyes on me like that.

Stumbling forwards, I brace my hands on the curved lip of the bar and lean over it towards the young, male bartender, exposing my ample cleavage.

"There's a rumour going around that you're serving rosé with gold flakes in it. Can I get one of those please?"

The bartender frowns and tilts his head. He opens his mouth to respond but Mr Sainz turns to face me and places his glass on the bar.

"I heard that too. Can you make it two of them, please?" His voice is rich and deep. My stomach turns over.

The bartender gives a nod and moves away to make the drinks.

I turn sideways, intent upon continuing the

charade, and fix a tipsy smile onto my face.

"Why, thank you. I don't think he knew what I meant until you stepped in."

He gives a slight shrug. "People usually seem to go out of their way to give me what I want."

"Oh? And why would that be?" I lean in and touch his forearm, dialling up the flirtation. My stomach is doing somersaults but I ignore it.

He leans closer and lowers his voice, "Perhaps because I pay them to."

I allow my face to morph into a look of surprise, swiftly followed by one of mortification.

"Oh my goodness. You're Nicolas Sainz." I press a hand to my open mouth and look away briefly before looking back up at him. "I'm sorry, sir. I didn't recognise you. The mask—"

He lets out a throaty chuckle. "No problem."

"I'm Holly Harrington, sir. I work for you. I'm sorry." I fake a sobering-up and offer him my hand. He takes it and shakes it gently, his hold on my hand lingering.

"Nice to meet you, Holly."

The bartender returns and places two glasses of rosé with gold flakes floating in them in front of us. Given that I fabricated the drink as part of my ruse, I'm impressed.

Mr Sainz reaches into his pocket, pulls out a gold money clip loaded with neatly folded fifty pound notes. He tugs one note free, folds it again and slips it to the bartender, who cocks his eyebrows before pocketing the tip.

"Wow," I whisper. "Quite a tip."

"I like to reward the people who go out of their way for me. You know? The nice people." The thick wad of cash has already disappeared back into his pocket. He lifts his glass and holds it up towards me. I hurriedly lift mine and clink it against his. "Cheers."

"Cheers. And Merry Christmas," I reply.

He nods and we both take a sip.

"So, tell me, Holly, have you been naughty or nice this year?"

I splutter on my drink and quickly try to recover.

"Erm, well, that depends. What do you do to the naughty people?"

He presses his lips together to mask a smile.

"I certainly wouldn't ask them to dance. Do you deserve a dance with the boss, Holly?"

The way he says my name makes me melt inside. The music the band is playing suddenly filters into my consciousness. I fight against rolling my eyes. It's "Run Rudolph Run". Claire's broken reindeer flashes through my mind.

"If I said no, I'd be giving too much away. But something tells me the same is true if I say yes." I stall for time and take another sip of wine.

He fixes me with his cool, grey gaze, head slightly tilted, assessing me.

The music shifts into a slow ballad and it takes me a few seconds to place it without lyrics to guide me. It's *that* song. The ultimate Christmas love song; "All I

Want For Christmas Is You".

My boss takes the glass from my hand and places it on the bar beside his own, he does the same with my precious clutch and I open my mouth to object, but he gives the bartender a single nod and he swoops in to move our things securely behind the bar.

"Dance with me." It isn't a question.

He takes my hand and leads me into the crush of bodies. The band's rendition of the song is slow and rich, strings and brass blending into a rhythm that slides straight under my skin. My pulse thrums to match it. His hand is warm, his palm steady against mine, and when he draws me in, my whole body fits against his like it's meant to be there.

The scent of him—cedar, leather, a trace of smoke—wraps around me. His other hand settles at the small of my back, firm enough to guide, not enough to trap. Still, I feel caught.

We move together easily, too easily. My heels scrape the floor once before I find his rhythm, and then I'm following it, melting into it. The world narrows to the glide of his body, the slide of velvet against wool, the faint scrape of stubble when he leans close enough that his breath grazes my ear.

"I see through your mask," he murmurs. "It's slipping."

I don't reply, I keep my gaze fixed just over his shoulder. I don't trust my voice not to betray me. His breath is warm on my neck and a tingle rushes up my spine.

He laughs softly, the sound vibrating through his

chest and into mine. "Mmm. You play at being unreadable, Miss Harrington, but you're an open book to the right reader."

The music swells; he turns me beneath his arm. My skirt fans out and his hand catches my waist again, drawing me back in, closer than before. My breasts brush his chest, and I can't pretend the heat between us is anything but real.

My heartbeat climbs into my throat. Every nerve is tuned to him—the strength of his hand, the slide of his thumb tracing the line of my spine, the faint pressure of his thigh against mine as we move. The room could burn down around us and I might not notice.

His hand travels upward, fingers sifting into my hair until his palm rests at the nape of my neck. It's a startlingly intimate gesture and I look into his eyes, drawn by the gravity in his gaze. His mask conceals his brow and many of his micro-expressions, but his eyes alone are piercing and they sear right into me. They're the colour of storm clouds over steel, and they hold me utterly still.

"You've been naughty," he says softly. The words hum against my skin. "Haven't you?"

The song slows, dissolving into its final refrain. He doesn't let me go. His thumb strokes the nape of my neck in a motion so tender it almost hurts. My breath catches; my whole body leans into him, waiting—for a kiss, a reprimand, I don't even know which.

"I see everything, Miss Harrington."

And just like that, he releases me. One moment he's there—heat, scent, pressure—and the next, he's gone, swallowed by glittering masks and bodies moving in time to a new song.

I stand in the middle of the floor, dizzy, weightless. The air feels too thin, my chest too light. When I finally glance down, my hand flies to my throat.

My pendant is gone.

Shit.

CHAPTER FIVE

I slip off the dance floor, lungs burning, the ghost of Nicolas's hand still pressed to the back of my neck. The pendant should be warm against my chest, a steady weight. Instead, my skin is bare, light, empty.

I drift toward the Christmas tree, using its massive shadow as cover. The thing towers over me, branches dripping with glass baubles and scarlet ribbon, twinkling lights throwing fractured colour across the wooden floor. Couples circle past in laughter and sparkle, too busy with each other to notice me clinging to the edge of the celebration.

That's when I feel it—a presence at my shoulder.

"You weren't answering your phone."

The voice is smooth, unhurried, and it scrapes down my spine like a blade.

I glance sideways, pulse thudding.

He's tall and lean, dressed head-to-toe in charcoal

grey. His mask is deep crimson, glossy as blood, covering half his face but leaving his mouth visible. Designer stubble lines his jaw.

My stomach hollows. I've never met him in person. He's always been a faceless entity behind the screen of my burner phone.

"I don't have it on me," I reply, frost on my tongue. We don't look at each other, both feigning an interest in the dancers.

He turns and tilts his head to look up at the gold star blinking at the top of the vast tree.

"What happened?"

My throat works around a lie, but there's no point. He'd see straight through it.

"Sainz took it." The words scrape out, barely a whisper.

His hand shoots out, fingers clamping around my upper arm. The grip is iron, cruel. Pain sparks white-hot under his thumb as he squeezes hard enough to bruise. I hiss between my teeth but don't pull away. That would be worse.

"You know what's at stake," he murmurs, close enough that only I can hear him. His breath smells faintly of mint. "Fix it. Or your parents pay the price."

I nod, quick and shallow, because words won't come.

He releases me at last, the ache blooming hot under my skin. His hand trails down my arm as if smoothing away the violence, but it's no comfort. "Good girl," he says softly. Then he fades back into the swirl of masks and sequins, vanishing like smoke.

I stand frozen, clutching my arm, breath shuddering in and out.

Above me, movement stirs on the mezzanine.

Nicolas Sainz.

He walks with quiet purpose toward the double doors of his office, dark tuxedo a cut of shadow against the glass. My stomach flips. He has my pendant. He has the file. He has everything.

And then another thought slices in, desperate, reckless.

Marcus.

If I can't reach Nicolas directly, I can use Marcus. His office. His access. His weakness.

I square my shoulders, fix a smile that feels like broken glass, and head back into the crowd in search of the VP. I go via the bar and retrieve my drink and clutch as cover while the band plays a swinging version of "Wonderful Christmas Time". I find Marcus holding court with a bunch of clients and insert myself into the circle around him, close enough to catch his eye.

The group laughs, that haughty fake kind of laughter found at functions like these. I press my lips together and fix a steady gaze on Marcus. He's laughing too, his eyes watering slightly, but the laughter dies on his face as his gaze meets mine. Something darker crosses his tanned skin.

Someone else picks up the conversation and it goes on around us. I hold his gaze, willing him to make a move. The heat radiating off him is painfully obvious to me and I wonder if anyone else senses it.

Marcus cuts across the group, ignoring the bony woman next to him who is trying to make a joke and making a pig's ear of it. He reaches for my hand, takes it and leads me away without a word. I fall into step just behind him, our hands swinging loosely between us. He comes to a halt near the edge of the dance floor.

"Back for more?" he says, shamelessly looking me up and down.

"Well, you said you weren't finished with me. I thought I'd give you a chance to show me what you meant." I take a sip of my gold-infused wine. The flakes have all settled in the bottom of the glass, so it's really just normal rosé now.

He moves closer, one hand snaking around my waist and resting on my back. I look up at him and flash him a smile.

"Are you sure?"

I nod and place my wine down on the tall table next to us.

"Alright then." He takes my hand again and leads me towards the door up to the executive offices. I'm all too aware that the security guard will probably recognise me. This could raise a red flag, but I have to try. It's too important.

Marcus pushes open the door and marches along the corridor towards the stairs. The door to the security office opens but Marcus waves a hand in the direction of the guard and waltzes right past him. I scurry along on my toes and giggle tipsily. I don't even get a look at the guard before the door closes again.

As we approach his office, he pulls his access card out of his pocket and I play the game.

"Oh, good, you found it!" I blurt out, too loudly in this quiet corridor. He glances my way, smirking.

"I did. No harm done."

"Phew." I blow a strand of loose hair with my heavy exhale and that elicits a light laugh from him. He taps the access pad and opens the door.

The low lights fade up as we enter. I didn't have the chance to look around earlier, so I allow myself to scan the room now, eyes wide with almost genuine wonder. It's sparsely furnished, but the far wall is entirely glass and London sparkles below us.

"Wow," I say, heading towards the window.

Marcus catches my hand and yanks me back towards him. He spins me and pulls me against his chest. I giggle, but inside I'm a reeling mess. He clamps a hand around the back of my neck and hungrily plants his open mouth on mine, forcing a rough kiss on me.

I let it happen. I have to. This is my opportunity. I let him think he's winning.

He backs me into the large desk that dominates the centre of the room and I whimper into his mouth as my backside collides with the wooden surface.

His hands grope at my hips and I know he's not wasting any time here, so neither can I.

I reach behind me, fumbling for what I need. There. My right hand bumps into the cool bronze bull paperweight. I grasp it just as I pull my head back for air. I grin at him as he loosens his tie then swing that lump of metal right at the side of his head.

It lands with a heavy *thunk* and he staggers sideways, then crumples to the floor.

I drop the paperweight beside him and step over him. I crouch down and quickly search his pockets for his pass. I grab it and dash out of there, running straight across the hall and tapping the card to the pad next to Nicolas Sainz's door. The light blinks green and I push the door open.

Sainz looks up at me from the other side of the desk, his mask discarded beside his keyboard and his hair slightly mussed. A deep frown creases his brow.

Behind him is a huge, curved glass wall displaying all of London's most prominent landmarks, all lit up for the festive season. His office takes up the entire width of this end of the oval-shaped building and it's breathtaking. But I quickly recover myself and glare at him.

"I need my pendant back," I say, stepping into the room. "Please."

He lifts his hand. Dangling on its gold chain is the pendant.

"This one?"

"Yes. You stole it. I need it back."

He tilts his head and purses his lips. Without a word, he lifts the gold cylinder and tugs the two sections apart, revealing the USB stick.

"And what did you steal with it first? What's on here, Miss Harrington?"

I try to find a quick retort, but nothing comes and I

just stand there with my mouth hanging open.

Sainz rounds the desk and stalks towards me. He glances past me through the open door, then down to the pass in my hand.

"Is Marcus alright?"

I shrug.

His gaze rakes up my bare arm and lands on the purpling skin of my upper arm. He gently lifts my arm by the wrist and his cheeks fill with colour. "Did he do this?"

I shake my head. "Someone much more dangerous did. That's why I need that pendant. I have to give them what they want. Please. You don't understand what's at stake."

He releases my arm, closes the door and leads me to the chair in front of his desk. Numbness fills my body as I drop into the leather chair. I've been on my feet for hours, aside from the brief interlude tucked under Marcus's desk.

"Tell me, Holly. Who are you working for?"

"Just you," I lie. Even though it's pointless.

He leans against the desk just to the side of me, his hands clasped neatly in front of him, my gold chain woven between his fingers.

"The truth, this time."

I take a breath and look up at him.

"An organisation called DUSK. And if I don't slip that USB stick to their operative downstairs in the next few minutes, my parents will lose everything that you didn't already take from them."

CHAPTER SIX

Nicolas blinks and tilts his head.

"Excuse me? What did I take from your parents?"

"Well, not you personally, but this company. They took bad advice and it landed them in terrible debt. Their house is at risk." A tear prickles at the corner of my eye. I swipe the ridiculous mask off my face and toss it onto the floor. I push anger to the surface to overwhelm the fear and sadness that I'd rather not show in front of him.

"I see." He raises a hand to his face and rubs it along his jaw and around to the back of his neck. "And DUSK stepped in? Bought the debt?"

"Yes."

"What did they want, Holly?"

"Information. If I give it to them they'll clear my parents' debt." My cheek twitches, tears still burning close to the surface.

"And you've been digging, haven't you?"

"Yes." Why am I being so honest with this man? I clam up. I've already said far too much.

"What's on this?" He holds up the pendant.

I don't want to say. A sharp pain stabs at my chest. But his gaze is sharper and I cave.

"A client list. Special projects. Something to do with something called Halcyon."

Nicolas's skin pales. He looks away.

"That's as far as you looked?" he asks, still not looking directly at me.

"Yes."

"Whose advice did they take? Your parents?" He leans a little closer, his voice low and softer than I deserve.

"Marcus Blythe's." The name is like acid on my tongue.

"Of course." Nicolas immediately springs into action. He pockets my pendant, rounds the desk and taps his keyboard. When he looks back at me a tear spills down my cheek and I swat it away. He glances past me to the door. "Right." Resolve crosses his face. He unfastens his tie and returns to my side. "Sorry about this, but you're a flight risk."

I open my mouth to object but he's not wrong. My pulse flutters anyway. He takes my wrists and presses them together against the padded arm of the chair, then winds the tie around them. The silk slides over my skin, whispering as it tightens. It's absurd, but my body registers it less as a restraint and more as a caress—soft where his grip is firm. The knot pulls snug, tethering me to the chair in a way that makes heat coil low in my stomach. I could fight, maybe even wriggle free if I tried hard enough, but I don't. The knowledge that I could but don't makes my breath come faster.

A reckless quip teases the edge of my tongue—something about ties and kinks—but I bite it back. Wrong time. Wrong man. Or maybe the right man at the wrong time.

He lingers just a second too long, fingers brushing the silk as if testing the knot—or testing me. Then he straightens, smooth and unreadable, as though he hadn't noticed a thing.

"I'll be right back." He stalks from the room and I swivel in the chair to see him disappear through the door and cross the hall to Marcus's office.

Frustration bubbles beneath my skin and I strain to listen for any hint of what's happening. Low murmurs drift across the hall but I can't make out what's being said. It seems as though Marcus may be conscious. I kick at the floor and try to move the chair so I can see through the half-open door, but I'm in more danger of knocking the chair over than moving it. I could probably wriggle out of the restraint, but something stops me. I fall still and frown, examining my own thoughts. I don't want to disappoint him. He's been kind. I can't fathom why. He should be firing me, calling the police. Maybe he still will, he did tie me up. But I get the feeling he won't.

I crane my neck again just in time to see him emerging from Marcus's office. He sweeps back into the room and goes to the phone on his desk. He taps a single button and a soft ring ripples from the handset in the quiet of his office.

"Security to Marcus Blythe's office immediately, please. He'll need medical attention, but he isn't to leave. Not until I have another conversation with him."

I stare open mouthed at him as the person on the other end offers a reply that I can't hear.

"Be discreet, please. There's no need to disrupt the festivities downstairs. No police at this time, not until I sort a few things out."

I blink and close my mouth, confusion rushing though me with my pulse.

"He assaulted a member of staff, so yes, it is serious. Could you also contact Gavin at Steel Link and ask him to assemble a special team and call me on my personal number as soon as possible? Thank you." He hangs up the phone and fishes my pendant out of his pocket. I watch, mute, as he plugs the drive into his computer.

"What are you doing?" I ask at last.

"Removing the data you copied onto here."

"Oh. And Marcus?"

He looks at me, a dark shadow crossing his face.

"He didn't assault me. I told you. This bruise was someone else."

"Your handler from DUSK, right?"

I nod.

"I know, and we'll deal with that shortly, but Marcus has had this coming for a long time. I had words with him just this evening about his wandering hands."

Heat rises in my cheeks. "I heard."

His mouth twitches.

"I know."

I shift my weight and cluck my tongue. Of course he knows.

"His desk chair was moving as we entered his office and I saw your reflection in the window behind the desk." The smile cracks on his full lips then and I return it with a heavy scowl.

"And then you saw me come back to the party and knew exactly where I'd come from?"

"Precisely. I've actually been aware of your actions for a couple of months now. Security flagged it and I've been keeping tabs on you. That's why you were invited to this little shindig."

"Oh." I didn't expect that. My cheeks redden and I avert my gaze. I had been so cocky, so sure I was getting away with it.

"What happened over there?" He asks, looking up from his computer and crossing his arms. He's imposing, even across the desk. Tall and broad, dark-haired and those startling, grey eyes are so sharp.

"I manipulated him into bringing me upstairs so I could get in here. I let him kiss me, then knocked him out with his paperweight and stole his access card."

Nicolas presses his lips together and gives a single nod.

"My understanding is that you'd had a drink too many and that my former VP led you into a private room where he proceeded to take advantage of you. He hurt your arm and you defended yourself."

I open my mouth, frown, and close it again. Great. I've become a goldfish.

"Isn't that right? Isn't that what you're going to tell security when they get here?"

"Why are you doing this?" My voice feels too small.

"Because I understand why you did what you did. All of it and it's within my power to fix this for you." He crosses the room and bends over to untie my hands. I swiftly pull them to my chest and flex the wrists. The ache from being tied isn't too bad, but it's been a long night.

"And what about DUSK? I have to give them what they demanded."

"You'll slip them the drive. But it'll be blank. They won't know that right away. It buys us time."

Footsteps carry up the stairs and along the corridor. The outer door lock beeps and the security team sweep into the space between the two executive suites. Nicolas moves over to the door to greet them and give them more information.

I sit where I am for as long as I can take it, hearing the hushed conversation beyond the door.

"...Shaken, but she'll be alright." Nicolas's voice carries a little above the others.

I get to my feet and follow him out into the hall. Three security guards glance my way, one of them is the one that escorted me out earlier. He looks me up and down, his gaze lingering on the bruise on my arm.

One of the others is carrying a small medical kit and she heads into Marcus's office to check him over.

Marcus's grumbling voice spills out through the open door and I retreat back into Nicolas's office. I head behind his desk and see the open folder on his computer showing an empty flash drive. His plan could work. My desire to ruin his firm has diminished since he so firmly took my side in this. I remove the drive, click it back into the pendant and gather up the chain into my palm. I retrieve my clutch and go back out into the hall. Everyone is in Marcus's office now, with the door closed, except for the familiar guard posted at his door.

"Are you alright, Miss?" he asks, looking at my arm again.

I nod. "Fine. Or I will be."

"I apologise. I saw him leading you up here and didn't intervene." His face crumples for a moment but he swiftly recovers himself and looks away.

"It's okay. You couldn't have known."

He rolls his shoulders and shakes his head, still not looking at me.

"He has a reputation. It wasn't excusable to ignore it. I knew you were intoxicated."

Guilt churns at my insides. Marcus didn't do anything I didn't invite. Now he'll be branded a sex offender. Fuck. I shouldn't feel bad for him. He ripped off my parents. He leered and groped at me, he was grossly inappropriate in the office. He's getting exactly what he deserves.

"What?!"

My thoughts halt in their tracks as the door opens and Marcus's voice bellows out of it. Nicolas emerges and closes the door. His stern gaze falls on me and softens a touch.

"Thanks, Frank. I'll take Miss Harrington back downstairs. Can you see to it that all of Mr Blythe's access is revoked right away, please? He'll be escorted, quietly, from the building after our guests have left."

"Of course, Mr Sainz. And I'm sorry, sir. I already apologised to Miss Harrington, but I let you down too, sir. I saw them coming up here and didn't stop them."

"There's enough blame to go around here, Frank, don't take too much of it on yourself." Nicolas pats the guard on the shoulder then holds out a hand to indicate for me to go ahead of him towards the exit.

I go with him with a nervous glance over my shoulder at poor Frank. Nicolas holds the door for me and leads me back towards the party.

At the foot of the curved staircase he comes to a halt and I stop beside him.

"How good is their surveillance? Do they have eyes back here?"

"No. Not that I'm aware of. My handler keeps messaging me when he hasn't got eyes on me."

"Okay, good. Check your phone now."

I do as he says and pull my burner out of my clutch. There are a string of missed messages. The latest one reads *tick tock*. I show him and his cheek twitches.

"You have the pendant already, don't you?" he asks.

I open my palm and show it to him, the gold

glinting in the bright light of the corridor.

"You like to play seductress. Can you play for a little longer?"

"Maybe. I don't know—What do you have in mind?"

"The only conceivable reason for us walking out that door together after being back here so long is that we—"

"Oh. Yes, I suppose."

"That's how you got it back, correct?"

"While you were redressing yourself?" I ask, cocking an eyebrow.

"Seems plausible."

"Fine. I can pretend." A small smile quirks the corner of my mouth.

Nicolas places his hand on the small of my back and guides me to the door. He opens it and the party atmosphere splashes my face like warm water. The music is loud, the laughter and merriment louder still. The air is thick with the scent of alcohol and perfume.

Nicolas's hand remains on my back, a gentle touch that sends a tingle up my spine. He leans close to me and kisses my exposed shoulder. A tiny gesture, but if we're being watched, it should sell it. I pretend it doesn't stir something deep inside me.

I cast my gaze around the room and quickly find Daryl leaning against the bar. His masked face is turned towards us. He's seen. Good.

I turn my body slightly towards Nicolas and lift a hand to his shoulder, rising onto my toes to whisper in his ear.

"At the bar, charcoal suit, red mask."

"I'll keep an eye on you, but you'll be fine." His lips ghost over my cheek, he squeezes my empty hand, and then leaves my side. I watch him scoop up a glass of champagne from a passing tray and make his way to the stage. The band draws their song to a close neatly and a hush falls across the room.

Nicolas moves over to the microphone and every eye in the ballroom is on him. I tear mine away and look back over to the bar. Daryl is moving slowly through the crowd towards me. I set off towards him too, the pendant held loosely in my right hand.

"Good evening," Nicolas's voice rings out over the PA system and a chorus of replies fills the air. "I hope you're all having a wonderful time. Thank you all so much for coming. You all know I'm not one for the spotlight, so I'll keep this brief."

He pauses and a soft ripple of laughter passes through the crowd. Daryl is just a few meters away. We keep moving towards each other, weaving through the people standing still and staring up at the stage.

"I'd like to thank the events team for their hard work putting this all together. Great job, folks." He claps carefully around his glass and everyone responds with polite applause.

So close, almost there.

"The band, the caterers, the bar staff, you've all been amazing." More applause.

Daryl and I draw level, gazes not on each other, just two strangers passing in a crowd. I hold my right hand out slightly as we brush past each other. He scoops the pendant from it.

"Good work, Harrington." His voice is the slightest whisper. And then he's gone. Vanishing back into the crowd with the empty flash drive.

"And finally, thank you to all of the staff for all of your work this year. It is truly appreciated. There may be some changes coming after the holidays, but I want you all to know how valued you are. I want nothing more than for this firm to be known for its integrity, discretion, and loyalty."

I stop dead and turn to face him. The crowd is nodding and whispering around me.

Nicolas's eyes find mine and I give him a firm nod. He raises his glass.

"Cheers, everybody, Merry Christmas."

"Merry Christmas!" the crowd cheers out. People clink glasses, drink, hug each other.

When I look back up to the stage, Nicolas is already vacating it and the band launches into something upbeat—horns bright, bass thrumming, the kind of song everyone knows by heart. The crowd starts singing, a hundred voices rising in slightly off-key harmony.

I push through the crush, clutch tucked under my arm, searching for him. My pulse hammers. He's vanished into the sea of masks and glitter. I crane my neck, scanning for a flash of dark hair, a glimpse of that tailored jacket. Nothing.

Then—hands. Firm, warm, claiming. They close around my arms and spin me. I gasp, half a breath from shouting, before I'm pulled hard against a solid chest that smells of cedar and danger.

"Done?" he murmurs against my hair.

"Done," I breathe. "What now?"

He pulls back just enough to look at me, his grey eyes catching the light, the corner of his mouth twitching in something halfway between pride and desire. His hand slides to the back of my neck, thumb brushing my jaw, and I swear the noise around us fades to nothing.

Then his gaze lifts, just briefly—above us. My eyes follow. A thick sprig of mistletoe dangles from the chandelier, green and glossy, its white berries catching the light.

Of course.

When his gaze drops back to mine, he's smiling. Not the polite, public smile of a CEO. Something slower. Hungrier.

"Seems tradition demands it," he says, voice a low rumble.

My heart stumbles. "We wouldn't want to be rude."

His breath fans across my lips a moment before he closes the distance. The kiss is deep, consuming. The world tilts. My fingers clutch the lapel of his jacket as his mouth claims mine—firm, deliberate, unhurried. The taste of champagne and salt lingers on his tongue, and my knees almost give.

When he finally draws back, his lips graze my cheek, his voice a whisper meant for me alone.

"Merry Christmas, Miss Harrington."

CHAPTER SEVEN

Whispers, chuckles and a faint whistle interrupt us and I pull back, glancing at the dozen or so people around us who are unashamedly gawking at the big important CEO snogging an underling. When my gaze returns to Nicolas, he only has eyes for me, not a care for being seen.

His hands skim down my bare arms and he clasps my hands, leaning close to my ear. His breath is warm against the sensitive skin.

"That should help to sell your cover."

"Huh." My cover. That's all that kiss was. Disappointment floods my chest and I try to push it away.

Nicolas releases my left hand but keeps my right clasped and sets off past the dance floor with me in tow, tottering along in my high heels. It feels as though I've done a lot of that tonight. I've lost track of time. Despite only having a few sips of drinks here and there, I'm light headed, as if I've drunk too much. I need the night to be over. I need my parents to be safe.

A bright ring tone emanates from Nicolas's inside pocket and he comes to a halt, lifting the phone out. He glances at the caller ID and gives me a firm nod before jerking his head towards the double doors out to the lobby. He answers the phone as he strides for the doors and again I scurry after him.

"Gavin, hi, thanks for calling me." He pushes open the door and we step into the bright, cool area in front of the two sets of lift doors.

"I gather you've had trouble." The voice on the other end of the phone is fairly clear out here where it's quiet and I can't pretend not to listen. I'm right there. And this is my business.

"Indeed. Marcus Blythe is being dismissed as we speak. I'm afraid we have a leak and it needs urgent plugging."

"Understood. What do you need?"

"One of my staff has been approached by DUSK. They've been blackmailing her. I need a team on her parents at once." Nicolas turns to me and frowns. "Where do they live? Are they local?"

"Erm, yes, Southgate. They'll probably be asleep. I don't want them disturbed."

"Don't worry, the team will just keep an eye on the house. I don't expect anything to happen. DUSK threatened them financially, yes? Not physically."

I nod. But now I'm worried. Far more so than I was

before. He's concerned enough to bring in private security to protect them.

"Did you get that, Gavin?"

"I did."

"I'll message you the address. Can you get a team there within the hour?"

"Consider it done."

Nicolas ends the call and passes me the phone.

"Type in the address."

I try, but my hands are shaking.

"Don't worry, Holly." His voice is firm, commanding. I look up at him. "Everything is going to be alright."

I take a deep breath and swiftly type in their address before handing the phone back to him. A few taps later and my parents' fate is in the hands of his private security firm. He tucks his phone back into his inside jacket pocket and takes a steadying breath himself. His gaze settles on me and I look up at him. Relief mixed with exhaustion and a strange sense of surrender. So much has been taken out of my hands. I've always craved control but right now, I'm happy to give it all up. The weight of it has been too much.

"Are you okay?" he asks, moving closer.

The lift doors ding and glide open. A member of security steps out and greets us with a polite nod. Nicolas takes my hand again and leads me into the empty lift. The doors slide closed and he moves closer, cupping my cheek with his hand. I wilt into the gentle touch.

"That kiss wasn't just for cover, was it?" I ask, pain evident in my voice.

"Not on my part," he says, his voice soft. He steps closer, our bodies almost touching. He dips his head. His lips brush against mine, tender, expectant. I return the kiss, my body melting against his. My clutch drops to the floor with a thud. My hands thread through his thick, dark hair. His cling to my back. He presses me against the cool, mirrored wall of the lift and deepens the kiss. Our tongues press together just like our bodies.

His left hand moves down to my hip and slides over my round arse. He squeezes. I moan.

My hands roam down his chest and I push his tuxedo off over his shoulders. He releases my body to shake the garment loose and it pools on the floor behind him.

The lift has begun to move silently downwards and the sensation swoops through my body.

Nicolas spins us, barely breaking our frenzied kiss and re-pins me against the adjoining wall, just so he can reach the control panel. He pulls his face away from mine just long enough to hit the emergency break button. The lift glides to a halt and he's on me again, hitching my right leg up and hooking it around his hip.

I've never needed a release like I do right now. I frantically unbutton his shirt and find firm muscles under a fine layer of dark hair.

He hitches up my dress, his fingertips seeking out the smooth skin of my thighs.

His hand slides higher, over my hip, grazing the lace edge of my knickers. I gasp into his mouth, half from shock, half from desperate want. He takes the sound as invitation, deepening the kiss until I'm dizzy.

"Nicolas—" His name breaks from me in a breathless moan.

He growls softly, the sound vibrating against my lips, and presses harder into me, pinning me with his weight. His fingers toy with the hem of my underwear, not rushing, just teasing, claiming my nerves inch by inch. The silk of his tie still burns phantom heat on my wrists, and the memory makes me shiver. He notices — of course he notices — and his lips curl against my throat.

"You like that," he murmurs, low and dangerous. Not a question.

My head falls back against the mirrored wall. He can't read my thoughts, he doesn't know I was thinking about having my wrists tied. But what he's doing with his fingers is as much of a turn on as my own thoughts. "I... don't hate it."

His laugh is quiet, wicked. "Good." His fingers slip beneath the lace, rough knuckles grazing the most sensitive skin. The contact is feather-light but it wrecks me, a jolt that has me clutching at his shirt, dragging him closer, desperate.

"You're trembling," he says, his breath hot against my ear.

"Maybe I've been waiting all night for this."

He groans, a sound that's half hunger, half restraint, and his mouth claims mine again as his hand finally moves with purpose. My leg tightens around his hip, pulling him against me. His hardness presses into my thigh through the fine wool of his trousers, proof of his own unravelling.

The lift hums around us, a tiny, private box in a skyscraper full of strangers. Upstairs, the party rages on, but here it's just us: our gasps, our hands, the desperate friction of bodies colliding.

He kisses me like he's devouring me, like he's wanted this as long as I have. Every touch is a command, every caress a promise of what comes next. And for once, I don't want to resist. I want to give in.

His fingers slip deeper, teasing, circling, and I cry out against his mouth. The sound bounces off the mirrored walls of the lift, shame and need blurring until I can't tell them apart. He swallows every gasp, every moan, his tongue tangling with mine as if he can drink me down.

The lace of my knickers is no barrier at all. He pushes it aside and sinks two fingers inside me, firm and deliberate. I shudder, nails digging into his shoulders, head falling back with a sharp gasp.

"God, you're wet for me already," he growls, teeth grazing my throat. "All night you've been playing your little games, and now look at you."

"I—" The protest dies on my tongue, torn away by another thrust of his hand. My hips move without my permission, grinding down onto his fingers, chasing the friction. My leg tightens around him, desperate to keep him close.

He works me hard, precise, his thumb stroking that perfect spot until sparks explode behind my eyes. The tie on my wrists, the pendant stolen, the lies — it all dissolves into the raw, pulsing truth of this moment: I want him.

"Say it," he demands, voice dark velvet. "Say you need me."

"I need you," I gasp, broken, undone.

He growls low in his chest, dragging his mouth back to mine, kissing me like he owns me. His pace quickens, fingers pumping, thumb relentless, until the pressure builds impossibly tight. I'm lost, gone, clinging to him as though he's the only thing tethering me to the ground.

The orgasm rips through me, sudden and brutal, my cry muffled against his mouth. My whole body seizes around his hand, thighs trembling, pleasure sparking through every nerve. He holds me steady, murmuring against my lips, riding me through it until I'm shaking, boneless.

He eases his fingers out, slow and possessive, then slips them into his mouth, tasting me with a groan that makes heat flare all over again.

"Perfect," he says, grey eyes dark and hungry. "Better than I imagined."

I sag against him, panting, my face pressed to his chest. His heart hammers beneath my cheek, steady and strong.

My pulse is still ragged, my thighs trembling from the force of what he just gave me, when Nicolas cups my face and kisses me hard, almost punishing in its intensity. When he pulls back, his eyes are molten steel, his voice low and rough.

"Do you know what happens to the ones on my naughty list?"

Heat flares hot in my cheeks, but I can't look away. "No," I whisper.

His lips curve, wicked and deliberate. "They get on their knees and make amends."

The words spark through me, submission and desire tangled tightly. My legs are still unsteady, but I drop down, the cool floor pressing through the thin velvet of my dress. I tilt my head back, meeting his gaze as I slowly undo the button of his trousers.

"Good girl," he murmurs, voice thick with need.

The praise makes me ache all over again. My fingers brush against him and he's already hard, straining against the fabric. I free him, the weight of him heavy and hot in my palm. His breath catches, a sharp sound that makes me want to please him even more.

I stroke him once, twice, slow and teasing, and he groans, his hand braced against the mirrored wall. His other hand tangles in my hair, not forcing, just guiding, claiming.

"You're going to make it up to me," he rasps. "For every secret you tried to keep. For every risk you took without me."

I lean in and take him into my mouth, his taste sharp and intoxicating. His hips jerk and he curses under his breath, low and harsh. I set a rhythm, tongue circling, lips sliding, and his grip tightens in my hair.

"That's it. That's how a naughty girl redeems herself," he growls, his voice breaking on the edge of control.

The lift feels hotter, smaller, filled only with the sound of my wet mouth and his ragged breathing. His thighs tense under my hands, his control fraying with every flick of my tongue, every hollow of my cheeks.

"Holly..." My name breaks from him like a plea and a command all at once.

I suck harder, take him deeper, and he lets out a guttural groan that vibrates through me, low and primal. His hips thrust, sharp at first, then ragged, as though he's fighting for control and losing it to me inch by inch. His grip in my hair tightens, not cruel but commanding, holding me exactly where he wants me. I close my eyes, the taste of him flooding my tongue, the sound of his broken breaths filling my ears.

And God, the way he unravels under my mouth—it makes me ache. Every shiver in his thighs, every growl in his throat sends ripples of pleasure through me. My core pulses with fresh need. Heat coils low in my belly at the sound of his unravelling. I revel in it—the power of reducing this aloof, untouchable man to shudders and broken sounds. Each gasp, each curse he grinds out above me is mine, drawn from him by my mouth, my tongue, my surrender.

I hollow my cheeks, press deeper, and his composure shatters. He bucks, groans, rides the wave hard, spilling into me with a shudder that seems to shake the mirrored walls themselves. His hand tightens in my hair as though anchoring himself, and I close my eyes, swallowing him down, dizzy on the taste, the intimacy, the rawness of it.

When I pull back, my lips are swollen, my breath uneven. I look up at him, and the sight of his eyes—bright, wrecked, utterly focused on me—makes me feel claimed in a way no knot of silk ever could.

He strokes a hand over my cheek, his touch suddenly gentle again. "Very good," he whispers. "Definitely on the nice list now."

The compliment sends a molten rush through me. I smile, shaky but real, and rise slowly to my feet. He catches me against his chest, kissing me softly this time, like he's sealing something neither of us is ready to name.

The lift is still frozen in place, the world held at bay. Downstairs, Daryl waits, the danger hasn't gone — but here, in Nicolas's arms, I feel safe. Claimed.

And I know this is only the beginning.

CHAPTER EIGHT

Nicolas takes his time to redress himself while I gather myself and straighten my dress. I glance at my reflection in the mirrored wall. My lipstick is almost entirely rubbed off, so I quickly clean it off properly. Only once we're both presentable does he hit the button to resume the lift's course to the ground floor.

"Are you okay?" he asks, running a hand up my arm.

"More than okay," I say with a slightly dopey smile. He returns it with a dazzling smile of his own. Fuck me, he's gorgeous. I hadn't fully appreciated that before. His dark hair is thick and slightly wavy, with just a hint of grey beginning to come through. I know from my research that he's forty two, ten years older than me, but that doesn't matter so much. Never married. In fact, his dating life has barely stirred the tabloids, unlike many other wealthy bachelors. He's done an impeccable job of keeping his private life private.

He takes his phone out of his jacket pocket just as the lift doors open on the ground floor. We step into the cool lobby, all white polished tiles and glass frontage. There's a security guard behind the desk and a small group of party guests milling in their coats, waiting for taxis, perhaps.

"Frank," Nicolas says into his phone. "Can you ensure that everything gets dealt with up there, please? I need to take Miss Harrington home."

My head tilts and I lock my sights on him, frowning. I'm not sure I agreed to that, but I'm not complaining.

"Yes, she's quite well, thank you for asking. Is everything calm up there? Good, good. Okay. Well the party should be wrapping up soon, I doubt it'll give you any trouble. Thank you." He hangs up the phone and tucks it away. "Did you bring a coat?"

"Yes." I reach into my clutch and find my cloak room ticket. He takes it from me, takes my hand, and leads me around the desk to the cloakroom on the other side of the lobby. The smartly dressed woman takes our tickets and disappears to retrieve our coats without so much as a second glance at Mr Sainz. She probably doesn't realise who he is. I quite like that he has that degree of anonymity. I'd hate to be recognised everywhere I go.

"You shouldn't go home," he says under his breath to keep his voice from travelling to the people standing behind us by the doors.

"No, I thought that too. They might know by now that it's blank."

"Quite. Would you be prepared to come back to my place with me?" His cheeks flush, which is adorable.

The coat-check woman returns with our coats and passes them to us over the desk.

"Yes. I think that would be best," I say, hiding a smirk as I slide into my long, burgundy coat.

Nicolas moves over to the reception desk, leans across it slightly and speaks softly to the guard. "Hi Pete. Would you have my car brought around, please?"

"Of course, Mr Sainz." The guard picks up the phone and Nicolas returns to my side. The people near the door glance our way at last just as he wraps his arms around me, drawing me against his firm chest. I smile, my face hidden from view. I could get used to this.

Before I can, though, he pulls away and leads me towards the exit. The revolving doors sigh open with his touch and a sleek black car glides to a halt at the kerb. It's not a gaudy supercar, not the kind of thing paparazzi would chase, but there's no mistaking the quiet opulence of it. Glossy paint, purring engine, tinted windows. The driver hops out, tall and neat in a dark overcoat, and sweeps open the rear door with a bow of his head.

Nicolas places a hand on my lower back as he guides me to the open door and I slide in first. The leather interior is warm, fragrant with polish and something sharper—mint, maybe. He joins me, and the driver shuts us into a cocoon of silence.

The city unfurls around us as we pull into the December night. Streets glitter with fairy lights strung across lampposts, shop windows glowing with tinsel and gold. London is festive, bustling, unaware of the danger pressing in on my ribs like a vice.

"You're quiet," Nicolas murmurs, watching me instead of the passing lights.

I turn my gaze from the window, meet his storm-grey eyes. "I keep expecting another message."

He nods at my clutch. "Check."

I fish out the burner, thumb the button. The screen glows cold blue, blank. No new threats. No demands. Just silence. Which is somehow worse.

"Nothing," I whisper.

Nicolas leans back, his jaw tight. "They won't give up that easily. But they've been outmanoeuvred tonight. That buys us time."

"Time isn't enough," I say, sharper than I mean to. My parents' faces rise unbidden—Southgate, their cosy house, the garden they've tended for decades. "DUSK will keep pushing until they get what they want."

His hand brushes over mine, steadying, grounding. "Then we make sure what they want never reaches them. And in the meantime, you are not alone in this. Do you understand me?"

I nod, though the words knot in my chest.

"Why are you helping me? You don't even know me?"

"I'm good at reading people," he says with a slight shrug. "I was moved by your situation and I can tell you aren't a bad person. You were doing what you felt you had to do. But I can provide another way out of it, so I will. And I take responsibility for Marcus." His VP's name is sharp on his tongue and his lip almost curls.

"Well, I appreciate it more than I can say. It's worth more than what we did in that lift." A smirk tugs at the corner of my lips and he nods, wetting his lips in response.

"I don't need any repayment. That certainly isn't how I view what we did."

I smile, my cheeks ache slightly. It's been a long evening.

The car slips through the city like a shadow, and soon we're pulling into a private drive. Discreet security gates swing wide, shutting out the chaos of London as we ascend into another world.

When the car stops, the driver opens the door and I step out into a quiet, floodlit courtyard. Glass and steel rise above me, gleaming against the night sky. Nicolas guides me to a private lift and swipes a card. The doors close and we shoot upward, faster and smoother than any building I've ever set foot in. My ears pop. My pulse does too.

When the lift opens, the world explodes into light.

I step out and stop dead.

The penthouse is like walking into a dream. Double-height ceilings soar above me, a wall of glass looking out over the sprawl of London—an ocean of lights glittering to the horizon. Velvet sofas in deep blue sit like jewels around a polished black coffee table. Silver sculptures catch the glow of recessed spotlights. Beyond, through folding glass doors, I glimpse a vast terrace with dining space and trees in planters, like a slice of luxury suspended in the sky.

My breath catches. I've seen wealth before, but nothing like this. Not lived-in, not intimate.

I glance at Nicolas, still by my side, watching me with that cool intensity. "This... this is your home?"

He tilts his head slightly, as though amused by my awe. "It is. Do you approve?"

I laugh softly, the sound too small for the space. "Approve? Nicolas, I feel like I've just stepped into a magazine spread."

"Good." His lips curve, the faintest smile. "Because for tonight, it's your home too."

I shrug out of my burgundy coat, suddenly too warm in all this opulence. Nicolas steps closer, sliding it from my shoulders with an ease that makes my breath catch. His touch is barely there, just a brush over my arms, but it leaves a trail of heat. He drapes the coat neatly over a chrome stand by the door, as if even that simple act has a ritual.

"Make yourself at home," he says, gesturing through the space. His voice carries like velvet through the high-ceilinged silence.

I don't move. My heels feel glued to the floor, dwarfed by the cavernous expanse.

He notices. Of course he does. "Come." His hand extends, palm up, steady, waiting.

I take it.

He leads me across the living space, past the sweeping glass wall and its glittering view of London, into a kitchen that gleams like a showroom. White marble counters, brushed steel appliances, cabinets that hide their handles like secrets. The place smells faintly of citrus and something woodsy—him.

Against one wall, a built-in wine rack rises in a geometric grid of dark wood, half-filled with bottles that look far too expensive for me to touch.

He studies the labels for a moment before selecting one, his movements unhurried, assured. "You like red?"

"Yes," I breathe, watching him with a strange mix of nerves and comfort.

He selects a bottle with care, uncorks it with smooth efficiency, and pours two generous glasses. The sound of the liquid against glass is oddly intimate in the hush. He hands one to me and lifts the other in a quiet toast.

"To surviving the evening."

I huff a laugh, clinking my glass to his. "Barely."

We sip. The wine is rich, like velvet on my tongue, and the alcohol slides warmth into my chest, loosening the knot of nerves. I lean a hip against the counter, holding the glass between both hands.

For a moment, there's no DUSK, no threat, no ledger hanging over me. Just him, standing a few feet away, sleeves rolled back to reveal strong forearms, the knot of tension finally slipping from his posture.

"You keep surprising me," I say before I can stop myself.

His grey eyes flick to mine. "How so?"

"You're..." I search for the right word, swirling the wine in my glass. "Not what I expected. I've been watching you for two years—at a distance, I mean. And you were just this... phantom. Power in a suit. Numbers on a page. I didn't expect you to..." I trail off, embarrassed, and take another sip.

His mouth curves, not quite a smile. "To be human?"

Heat rises to my cheeks. "Something like that."

He steps closer, slow, deliberate, until the edge of his hip brushes the counter beside mine. His glass rests on the marble with a soft clink.

"And what do you see now, Holly?"

The sound of my name in his voice makes my pulse stumble. I should look away. Instead, I meet his eyes. Grey and sharp, yes—but not cold. They're searching, vulnerable in a way I've never seen from anyone in his position.

"I see a man who tied me to a chair with his tie," I say, teasing just to break the tension.

A low chuckle escapes him, the sound dark and warm. "And you didn't run when I let you go."

"No," I admit, my smile slipping. "I didn't."

For the first time all night, I feel the tension bleed from my body, replaced by something deeper, steadier. Not just adrenaline, not just lust. Trust. Dangerous, impossible trust.

The wine warms a path down my throat, steadying the storm that's been raging inside me all night. I set my glass carefully on the counter beside his, afraid my hands might tremble if I hold it too long. Nicolas looks so comfortable, one hand resting on the marble counter by his wine glass, so at home. The stiffness is gone from his shoulders.

"It's not often I bring someone here," he says. His tone is casual, but there's weight beneath it, as though he's offering me a truth people don't usually get to hear.

I glance around at the gleaming kitchen, the sheer impossible luxury of it all. "I can see why. Most people would never want to leave."

His mouth quirks, but his eyes stay serious. "It gets lonely, sometimes. Quiet." He swirls his wine, gaze fixed on the dark liquid. "I built a life where no one gets close enough to do any damage. Useful, yes. But... empty."

The confession presses at something inside me, a mirror of my own hollow places. "I know the feeling. Different circumstances, but... yeah. Empty is a word I know too well."

He looks up at me then, and for a moment there's no CEO, no Systems Coordinator, no threat of DUSK— just two people, standing in the soft light of a penthouse kitchen, seeing each other.

The air hums with the weight of it.

I take another sip, mostly to hide the way my throat feels suddenly tight. "So," I say lightly, "am I here to keep you company, then?"

His smile deepens, softer this time. "You're here because I don't want you anywhere else."

The words hit me square in the chest, knocking my breath sideways. I laugh, too quickly, a little shaky. "Careful, Nicolas. That almost sounded like charm."

"Not charm," he says, his voice lower now. "Truth."

The space between us feels smaller with every

heartbeat, even though neither of us has moved.

I raise my glass again, but Nicolas beats me to it, sliding it gently out of my hand and setting it beside his. He doesn't break eye contact.

His voice is low, quiet enough that it feels like it's only for me. "Earlier, in my office... when I tied you to that chair."

Heat flickers low in my belly. My lips part, but no words come.

"Did you like it?" he asks, tilting his head, watching me with those piercing grey eyes. "Even just a little?"

The air thickens, heavy with tension. My mind scrambles for denial, for something clever, but my body betrays me—pulse racing, thighs pressing together, a warmth curling in places I don't want to admit.

"I—" My voice cracks. I swallow, trying again. "It was... unexpected."

He smiles, slow and devastating. "That's not what I asked."

My breath stutters. I could lie. I should lie. But the truth rushes up before I can stop it. "Yes."

The word hangs between us, charged, dangerous.

Nicolas steps closer, his hand bracing against the counter beside my hip. His scent surrounds me, subtle spice and expensive cologne, undercut with something uniquely him. His mouth hovers inches from mine, not kissing, just close enough to scorch.

"You have no idea," he murmurs, "how badly I want to test just how much you liked it."

My knees threaten to give way. The world narrows

to the heat between us, the quiet thud of my heartbeat against the marble stillness.

He holds my gaze a moment longer—long enough for me to forget how to breathe—then something in his expression shifts. Controlled. Decisive.

"Come," he murmurs.

CHAPTER NINE

His words are still echoing through me as Nicolas pushes gently away from the counter, reclaiming my hand with effortless authority. The wine, the marble kitchen, the safety of small talk—it all feels like a flimsy prelude now.

I let him lead me out of the kitchen and down the wide hall, past sleek panels of glass and art that probably costs more than my yearly salary. My heels click against polished wood until we emerge into the living room.

The city yawns out before us, endless lights shimmering through the floor-to-ceiling windows. London looks like it's holding its breath. My reflection stares back at me—flushed cheeks, red hair tumbling wild, eyes far too wide.

Nicolas releases my hand only to slip out of his jacket, tossing it over the back of the sofa with casual precision. He doesn't look at me when he does it, but I feel the weight of his attention all the same.

"This view," I whisper, as though I need an excuse for my nerves.

"This view," he repeats, but his gaze is on me, not the skyline. He steps closer, close enough that the warmth of his body prickles across my skin. His fingers trail lightly along my hip, then skim upward, brushing the bruise on my arm. Possessive. Protective. Both at once.

"Here," he murmurs, turning me gently until my back meets the cool glass. "I want to see you like this."

Nicolas lifts one hand, brushing a strand of hair from my cheek. His touch is soft, reverent, and yet the tension in his body tells me he's holding something back. My pulse thrums in my throat.

"You're trembling," he whispers, fingertips gliding down my bare arm.

"Because of you," I breathe, and it's the truth.

His palms return to my waist, lingering at the velvet fabric of my dress.

"Let me see you."

My breath hitches as he finds the hidden zip at my side. He doesn't rush, easing it down inch by inch, the sound almost scandalous in the hush. The fabric loosens and his fingers graze the warm skin of my ribs. My body arches into his touch, betraying me.

The dress slides down, velvet whispering against my thighs, until it pools at my ankles. I stand in my heels and lingerie, the glass cool and unyielding at my back, Nicolas's heat blazing at my front.

He takes his time. His hands trace the curve of my hip, the dip of my waist, the swell of my breast. Every stroke leaves sparks under my skin.

Inside my head, everything is chaos. This is reckless, dangerous, forbidden. He's my boss. He's holding secrets that could ruin me. And yet every part of me is screaming yes.

Nicolas leans down, his lips grazing the hollow of my throat, sending a shiver skittering down my spine. His breath is warm, his stubble a delicious scrape.

"Beautiful," he murmurs against my skin. His teeth catch lightly, and I gasp. My palms flatten against the cold glass, seeking balance.

His thumbs tuck into the elastic of my underwear and he nudges it down over my hips. The lace garment slides to the floor. His hands run up my sides and around to my back, arching me away from the glass enough to unhook my strapless bra, which he tosses aside.

"Perfect," he whispers, his lips ghosting over my collarbone.

His hands go to his waist. A slow tug, a soft whisper of leather sliding free from his belt loops. The sound makes my stomach swoop.

"You said you liked being tied," he says, voice low, dangerous silk. "Let's see how much."

He wraps the belt around my wrists, binding them together. My breath hitches as he tightens the leather and fastens the belt. He steps back and drinks in my naked body as he unfastens his shirt and slips out of it.

Self-conscious, I wait, my legs shaking slightly. My feet ache from my shoes and it's icy cold here against the glass, but I'm determined to be good for him. So I wait.

Nicolas drops his trousers and boxers, stepping out of them and kicking off his shoes. It's my turn to stare at his body.

He's in remarkable shape for a man his age. His muscles are well-defined. His tanned skin is covered in fine, dark hair. And his erect cock is a thing of beauty.

Standing there, breathless, I watch him reach for his discarded wallet and pull out a square packet. It's unexpected, grounding. But of course he would be prepared. Of course Nicolas Sainz would never leave something so important to chance. He slides the condom over his thick shaft and a wave of heat rushes through me, not dampening the moment but sharpening it, making me feel seen, cared for—even as I wait, bound and trembling.

He steps closer and threads his fingers through my thick, red hair. My bound hands can't help but take hold of him, gripping firmly and stroking the full length. He hums with pleasure as his lips plant kisses along my jaw.

Nicolas cups my right breast in his hand and rubs his thumb over the hardening nipple. His other hand slips between my thighs and his fingers pass over my clitoris, dragging a shaking breath from my lips. I'm already soaked and I grind my hips, pressing deeper into his hand, yearning for more.

"So eager, aren't you?" he murmurs against my throat.

"Can you blame me?" I ask, half laughing.

He pulls back and grins at me as he slides two fingers inside me.

My head bumps back against the glass. My legs are shaking. It's getting harder to stay on my feet. He must sense it because without a word, he scoops my bound hands up and hooks them over his head. He pulls his fingers out of me, grabs my thighs and hoists me easily up, pressing my back against the cool window.

I gasp as he enters me, one thick inch, then another, slowly lowering me onto him.

"Fuck," I whimper.

"Hmm. That feels so fucking good." His breath is warm on my face, the scent of the wine thick and intoxicating.

I can't breathe, can't moan. I press back against the window and close my eyes until he's sheathed all the way inside me. Good God, he fills me perfectly.

His mouth finds mine and his tongue probes hungrily as he begins to move in me. His fingers dig into the flesh of my thighs as he holds me in place and my skin squeaks against the glass as it warms with my body heat. I kick off my high heels and they drop to the thick carpet with a pair of light *thuds*.

Our hips rock in tandem and the way he moves his is expert-level fucking. There's a roll to it that hits every spot inside me with precision.

Pressure builds swiftly inside me, a deep sensation

in the pit of my stomach. It washes over me and a moan spills from my mouth, breaking our kiss.

"Fuck, Nicolas. Fuck!"

Before the wave even ebbs away, another one is crashing over me and I'm coming again. My muscles clench around him. With my wrists straining against the leather belt, I can't touch him. I can't even pat his back, or stroke his hair. I'm powerless. Somehow, that strikes me as even hotter and my climax is explosive.

Nicolas throbs inside me and his breath becomes short and desperate against my throat. He moans. His cock swells. And then we come together, groaning and thrusting our hips.

Our moans fade, our movements slow. Finally we fall still, me still pinned between him and the window. Our eyes meet and he kisses me, soft, tender, slow. He carefully unhooks my hands and pulls out of me, making sure the condom stays in place until he's all the way out of me. He lowers me gingerly to my feet. My legs give way, turned to jelly, and I collapse to the floor, giggling.

He drops to his knees and grasps my shoulders.

"Are you alright?"

"Perfect, thank you." I grin stupidly at him. "Do you mind?" I ask, holding out my bound hands.

Without a word, he unfastens the belt and swiftly unwraps it. He takes both of my hands and kisses the inside of each wrist in turn.

"That was incredible," he says at last, not quite meeting my eyes.

"It was amazing." I drop onto my side, the plush carpet soft and warm against my tingling skin.

Nicolas lays down facing me, his head propped up on his hand. His other hand caresses my side, sending little aftershocks through my nervous system.

For a moment we just lie there on the carpet, the city passing by beyond the glass, my skin still buzzing. His fingers trace absently along my ribs, but his eyes are far away, storm-grey and unreadable.

I break the silence first. "You spoke about them like you've dealt with DUSK before."

His gaze flicks to mine, sharp. "I've seen what they do. That's enough."

"That's not an answer."

"No," he agrees, voice flat. "It isn't."

I push up onto one elbow, suddenly restless. "So you know more than you're telling me. Why?"

"Because the less you know, the safer you are." His tone softens, but it doesn't make the words easier to swallow.

I huff out a humourless laugh. "Safe? You think I'm safe? They've got my parents under their thumb, they got me stealing from your company, and very soon they'll know I've been compromised. Safe isn't even in my vocabulary any more."

His jaw flexes. "You're safer with me than without me. That much, I can promise."

I want to believe him. God, I do. But I don't know this man. Not really. I only know how he feels pressed inside me, how he made my body betray every line I swore I wouldn't cross.

"What are you going to do?" I ask finally.

"That depends on how far DUSK is willing to go. And how far you're willing to trust me."

My throat tightens. "And if I don't?"

His smile fades. "Then they'll eat you alive."

The words hang between us, cold as the glass at my back.

"I want to trust you, but I don't know if I can."

"You can," he says firmly, his grey eyes like steel. "Because you already do." His thumb brushes the bruise on my arm, gentler than a breath. "You let me tie you, Holly. You let me see you like that. Don't pretend that wasn't trust."

Heat floods my cheeks, not from arousal this time, but from the truth of it.

"You make it sound so simple."

"It isn't." His voice drops. "But if you'll let me, I can simplify it for you."

"Why would you do that? We only just met."

"Because I have a good sense about people. I know you're a good person and right now you're in a challenging situation. It's possible you could get out of it yourself. I imagine you don't want a knight in shining armour to rescue you."

I try not to laugh. He's not wrong.

"But I hope to be able to prevent things getting far worse before they get better for you. It's within my power to do that. Besides," he says, caressing my shoulder with his finger tips. "I have my reasons for wanting to get in the way of DUSK's plans."

"Oh really?" I cock an eyebrow and lean closer. "Care to share those reasons?"

"Hmm," he leans closer still, his nose almost touching mine. "Maybe, if you continue to be a very good girl."

Our lips brush together and all I want in this moment is to be exactly what he wants me to be.

CHAPTER TEN

When a yawn I can't suppress breaks the comfortable silence between us, Nicolas is spurred into action. He helps me to my feet and scoops up all of my clothes and my clutch.

"Come on. Bed." His command is compelling and I take his hand. He leads me to the wooden stairs leading up to the second level of his penthouse, which overlooks the huge living area. We pass a neatly-appointed guest bedroom and continue to the end of the landing, where he opens the door on his bedroom. It's huge and my mouth goes dry just looking at it. It's as modern and polished as downstairs, but there's a warmth to it in the touches of wood; the burgundy and cream soft furnishings; and the scent of cedar in the air. The bed is enormous and stands against the far wall with a sleek, wooden headboard. To the right are two doors. I'd put money on them leading to a dressing room and bathroom.

For right now, my sights are set on that bed and the comfort it offers.

Nicolas places my things on a chair, my shoes beneath it, and pulls back the thick duvet.

"Make yourself comfortable," he says as he pads, naked, to the leftmost door.

With a grin, I run, like a little kid, over to the bed and jump into it. I snuggle in under the duvet and rest against the stack of thick pillows. I could get used to this.

A few minutes later, the door opens and I glimpse a brightly lit bathroom behind Nicolas as he slips back into the bedroom. He flicks off the light and climbs into the bed beside me, easing down and drawing me into his arms. I roll onto my side and spoon against him. The heat of his body envelops me and my eyes flutter closed.

All thoughts of DUSK, my parents' troubles, and everything that happened tonight, drift from my mind and sleep claims my aching body.

I wake to the cool light of day filtering through the curtains. I roll over and find myself alone. I sit up, rubbing my eyes. I look around for a clock and find one on the opposite night stand—10.30?—Far later than I'd have liked. A clink from downstairs alerts me to his presence in the apartment.

I look down at my hands and find dark smudges on them from my eye make-up. With a stab of guilt, I slip out of the bed and into the bathroom. The white tiles and glass surfaces gleam in the bright lights. I make use of the facilities, including thoroughly washing my face. It's awfully soon for Nicolas to see me without make-up, but it can't be helped. I'd far rather that than him see me with smudged, day-old make-up.

When I'm all cleaned up, I pad back into the bedroom and peek behind the other door. As I suspected, it opens on a large walk-in wardrobe filled with his suits, shirts, jeans, and everything else a wealthy man could need. I tug a light blue shirt off its hanger and slip it on, fastening the minimum number of buttons to preserve my dignity, if not my modesty. The hem brushes my thighs and the sleeves cover my hands. It'll do.

With an excited grin, I open the bedroom door and step onto the landing. I take two steps before I realise that the living room below, perfectly visible from the landing, is filled with people. A large Christmas tree now stands in one corner of the room, partially decorated, with three people still hanging baubles on it. Someone else is fastening a long garland to the glass banister ahead of me. Other people scurry back and forth below with boxes of decorations.

I tug at the shirt, wishing it was several inches longer. Or you know, my own clothes.

The man on the stairs glances my way but doesn't react to my presence, or my state of dress, in any discernible way. So I continue towards the stairs and pass him, an awkward smile brushing my lips, which he doesn't return.

"Denise, did you have a pastry yet?" a familiar voice calls from below.

I hurry down the stairs and through the bustling living room, into the kitchen, where the scent of fresh coffee and the sizzling of bacon in a pan greet me. The large island in the middle of the kitchen is laid with trays filled with croissants, pain-au-chocolate, doughnuts, and every other delicious breakfast pastry imaginable.

A woman with blonde hair in a tight bun bustles past me with a smile and helps herself to a cinnamon roll.

Nicolas turns to me from his place at the hob. Eggs are scrambling and bacon frying in separate pans and the toaster pops with several slices of golden toast.

"Good morning." He beams at me and moves around the island to greet me. He slips a hand around my waist and pulls me against his body. Our lips meet. His breath tastes of coffee. When he pulls away, he hums appreciatively. "I could get used to seeing you in my shirts."

I try to smile, but am all too aware of the people dashing about around us. I pat my bushy hair and tug the shirt to make sure it's covering my arse.

"I would have worn more if I'd known we had company."

"I'm sorry." He moves back to the hob and flips the bacon. "You were so tired. I wanted to let you sleep."

"It's fine. Thank you for that." I scoot myself up onto a high stool at the island and help myself to a croissant. It's still warm. "What is all this, anyway?"

He turns back to me, a spatula in hand. "Christmas." He answers like it's the most obvious thing in the world.

"This is just normal to you, then?" I ask, picking at the flaky pastry.

"Yes." He shrugs. "I love Christmas but rarely have time to decorate this place myself, so I have people come and do it for me. I would have had them in a week ago, but I was away until yesterday."

"Sure," I say, as if I know exactly what he's talking about. He watches me shrewdly and chuckles.

"Sorry. I forgot that you wouldn't know all my comings and goings. I was in St. Moritz for two weeks until yesterday afternoon."

"Wow. Lifestyles of the rich and famous, huh? You hopped on a plane and came straight to the masquerade?"

"More or less." He replies without reacting to my slight dig. He hands me a plate of bacon and eggs and silver cutlery. I take it with a smile and find a space on the island between the mountains of pastries. He joins me with his own plate and sits beside me, his knee bumping mine. A flutter rushes through my belly.

"This is perfect, thank you." My heart isn't quite in the words. A treacherous part of me is imagining him skiing and sipping champagne with glamorous blondes in Switzerland just days before screwing my brains out against his living room window. I wonder briefly how many conquests he has to his name and if I'm just a passing folly. One he'll regret by tomorrow. If so, is my job at risk when he gets bored with me?

As if reading my thoughts, Nicolas turns to face me and swivels me around on my stool to face him. He tucks a finger under my chin and tilts my face up so I'm forced to meet his steel-grey eyes.

"Holly, you are my priority. I will do everything I can to ensure your safety and security, and that of your parents. No matter where I was or what I was doing yesterday. My life has a lot of moving parts, but as of last night, you are the most important one."

"Okay," I say, my voice impossibly small.

He leans forward and kisses me, soft, tender, full of promise. I believe him. I return the kiss and slip my hands up over his chest and around his neck.

A throat clearing pulls us apart and a crisp voice calls from the kitchen doorway, "Mr Sainz, where would you like this?"

I glance over my shoulder and see the blonde woman holding up a large sprig of fresh holly. I return my gaze to him and smirk.

"Everywhere," Nicolas replies, his hands still resting just above my hips and his gaze not leaving my face. "Get more. I want holly all over this apartment."

I press my lips together and try not to laugh. The woman stalks away and Nicolas leans in to plant a soft kiss on my lips. His hands move to the tops of my thighs and his thumbs brush under the soft cotton of his shirt to stroke the creases where my legs meet my body. I hum appreciatively and steal another smouldering kiss. I part my knees and he runs a finger down to my clit. I gasp as he brushes over it. He breaks the kiss and looks into my eyes as he slowly slides his finger inside me.

A whimper escapes my parted lips and I flinch, acutely aware of the people bustling about the apartment just behind me. He isn't deterred. His finger slips deeper and begins to stroke the inside of my pussy. His other hand remains planted on my leg, holding me steady on the high stool.

"I want you," he whispers, his voice thick. "Right here. Right now."

"But your little helpers are still here," I whisper back, my nose tantalisingly close to his.

"I don't care. I pay them to be discreet."

I moan, low and deep in my chest as his finger presses harder inside me. My hands move down to the button of his jeans. I pop it and slide the zip down. I reach into his jeans and through the front opening of his boxers. He's already rock hard and straining at the cotton. I wrap my hand around his thick cock and start to tug it free when a bright ringtone fills the kitchen. I immediately release him from my grasp.

Nicolas groans and drops his forehead onto my shoulder. He lifts his head again and reaches into his back pocket, while still keeping his other hand where it is, his finger buried deep inside me.

"Sorry. I have to take this."

All I can do is nod. Fuck. What is he doing to me?

"Gavin?" He says into the phone on answering. His voice is cool and professional and totally at odds with our domestic bliss. His finger keeps rubbing the sensitive spot inside and my head drops back.

"They what?" His tone shifts and he swiftly slides his finger out. Suddenly empty, I look at him, a frown creasing my brow.

Nicolas reaches for a paper napkin from a stack on

the end of the island and wipes his finger on it.

"Right now? It might be nothing. Keep watch. I'll stay on the line."

"What is it?" I whisper, suddenly concerned.

Nicolas takes my hand and I scoot off the stool. He leads me swiftly through the living room and up the stairs. I stay close to the wall, anxious that the minions below might see up the shirt.

"Yes, I'm still here. Right. Hold on." He pushes his bedroom door open, leads me inside and closes it again with a soft click. He pulls the phone slightly away from his face and fixes his cool grey eyes on me. "Check your phones. Both of them."

I nod and hurry to my clutch on the chair. I dig out my own phone first. The battery is down to twenty percent, but there are no messages or missed calls.

"Is he still at the house?" Nicolas asks down the phone. I glance at him as I switch phones. He runs a hand through his thick hair. He looks worried.

"Nothing," I mouth, holding up my phone. Then I turn my attention to my burner. The battery is almost flat but it has enough power to tell me that I have a dozen missed calls and even more messages. All from Daryl. "Fuck."

Nicolas leans closer and looks at the phone's history.

"Okay. Hold fire. It might be nothing, but I'll get back to you if I learn anything. Thanks, Gavin." He hangs up the phone. "Call your parents, right now."

"Tell me what's happening." I glare at him, my

patience thin.

"It's probably nothing, but the security team surveilling your parents' house have seen a van pull up near the house. It's marked up like it's the gas company. It stayed parked for ten minutes before a man in overalls got out and went to your parents' door. He spoke to a man, presumably your dad, for several minutes then got back in the van. It's still parked there. You need to call your dad and find out what was said."

I nod, my hands are shaking. I bring up my parents' landline number on my own phone and hit the call button. It rings. And rings. I chew the inside of my cheek. Finally my mum answers with a bright "Hello?"

"Mum!" I reply, a little too eagerly.

Nicolas places a steadying hand on my shoulder.

"Hi, Mum. How are you?"

"Oh hello, Holly. Fine, thank you. How was your party last night?"

"Great. How's Dad?"

"He's fine." Caution slips into her voice. "Is something wrong, sweetheart?"

"No, I'm fine. And Dad's alright?"

"He's fine. I already said that."

"You did. Yes. What's going on there this morning? Anything interesting?" I try to sound casual but I know I'm failing miserably.

"No, nothing interesting. Holly? What's wrong?"

"Nothing. Can I say hi to Dad?"

"Of course you can, hold on." There's a pause and I

look helplessly at Nicolas. He squeezes my shoulder. "It's Holly. She wants to say hello." Mum's voice calls out at the other end of the line. I hear my Dad making shuffling noises as he comes to the phone. His hip isn't so good these days and he doesn't move about quickly.

"Hello, sweetheart. Everything alright?" he asks when he gets to the phone.

"Just great, Dad. How are you? How's your hip today?" I do a better job of playing it cool with him. My Dad has that effect on me. Soothing, comforting. He is my safe place.

"Oh, you know, same as ever. Can't complain."

"Well don't push yourself. No running to the door when the bell rings." I manage a small laugh to let him know I'm joking, but I'm doing my best to lead him to what I need to know.

"Hmph," he snorts. "I had to answer it just now, actually as your Mum was upstairs. It was just the gas board come to read the meter. Could have done that without ringing the bell. It's right there on the side of the house."

"Oh I know," I say, nodding and trying to sound sympathetic. "Did they need to talk to you?"

"Well, to be fair, yes, he said something about some work on the street and them needing to shut the gas off on Monday."

"Oh really? Did he say how long for?" I glance at Nicolas. He can hear every word. He waits patiently, far more so than me.

"A few days. I don't suppose you've got a camping

stove?" He chuckles.

"No, sorry. Not really my thing. But I can get you one and bring it over. Did he say anything else? The gas man? Was he friendly enough?"

"Friendly? Well, not really, he was professional enough. Odd fellow though. Had a scar on his cheek and very big, imposing. I felt a little uncomfortable to be honest. He kept me talking for longer than I'd like."

"I'm sorry, Dad." Nicolas and I exchange nervous looks.

"Not your fault, sweetheart. Tell me about your party. Was it as glamorous as you said it might be?"

"It was lovely, really special." I smile, trying to keep my thoughts on the task at hand and not what Nicolas and I did in the living room. Or the lift.

"Oh good. Did you dance with anyone special?" There's a grin in his voice and I bite back a laugh.

"Dad. Shush."

"Oh all right. But you know I'm keen to walk you down the aisle some day. You haven't been with anyone special since Theo."

"Dad. Please." My cheeks blaze and I turn away from Nicolas. "I have to go."

"Oh don't mind me, sweetheart. I'm just pulling your leg."

"No, you're not," I say in a tone of mock scolding. "But these things can't be rushed."

"I know. I know. Off you go then, have a nice weekend."

"I will. And Dad, if the gas man comes back before

Monday will you let me know so I can come down there and give him what for about bothering people on a weekend... At Christmas?"

He chuckles. "Of course."

"Say bye to Mum for me."

I hang up. Nicolas is already calling Gavin.

"It's something," he says as soon as Gavin answers. "By the sounds of it, they may be creating a cover to put in surveillance equipment. Can you keep a team on the house full time until further notice?"

I don't hear Gavin's reply.

"Is the van still there now?" He nods. "Right. Let me know when they leave. I'll be on my mobile all day."

He hangs up and drops his phone onto the bed.

"What do we do?" I ask, wiping my sweating palms on his shirt and immediately feeling bad about it.

"You need to reply to your handler. Let's try and do some damage control. There is every chance that you had no idea that drive was blank when you handed it over. Right?"

"Right."

I try to absorb his certainty, but the effect is fleeting. Anxiety gnaws at my insides. I have a terrible feeling that things are about to get much worse.

CHAPTER ELEVEN

"I need to go home. Right now." I start getting dressed in last night's clothes. "My phone battery died. That's why I didn't get all those calls and messages."

"Okay, yes. I'll drive you."

"No," I shake my head as I straighten my dress. "They may be watching my flat. I have to go alone."

"Holly—" He tries to object but I place a firm hand on his chest.

"Send one of your special security teams to tail me if you like, at a safe distance. But if DUSK are watching me, I have to appear alone."

"You're right. You book a taxi, I'll speak to Gavin." He marches from the room and I catch a few barked orders to the staff before he's out of earshot. I do as he says and book an Uber, cringing at the thought of how much it'll cost to get across London the Saturday before Christmas.

An hour later, I pull up outside my building and scoot out of the car. My flat is on the second floor of a converted terraced house in Stoke Newington. The newsagent across the road bustles with people coming and going and someone charges past me on the pavement wheeling a small suitcase behind them. I rush up the steps to the front door of the narrow terraced house. It looks about as run-down as every other house on the busy street and the sight of it brings me back down to earth with a thump.

An unremarkable, grey car parks opposite, a few doors down from the newsagent and I wonder if it's my security detail.

I unlock the door and step into the dark hallway, which is littered with discarded take away fliers and charity donation bags. Mr Gomolka's pit bull starts barking like crazy behind his door. I hurry up the stairs before my neighbour can stick his head out to corner me about my comings and goings. I find the key to my flat on the ring and unlock my door. The air behind me moves and a hand clamps around the back of my neck. I stifle a cry.

"Get inside, nice and calm now." Daryl presses himself against my back and something sharp pokes into my side.

Holding my breath, I open the door and step over the threshold into my living room. He keeps hold of me even as he kicks the door shut behind us.

"What's going on?" I ask, trying to stay calm, but my pulse is racing.

He lets me go and shoves me away from him. I

stumble on my high heels and take a moment to steady myself before whipping around to face him.

"I've been here for hours. Where the fuck have you been?"

"Who let you in?" I demand. I'm going to kill Mr Gomolka.

"Answer my question first. I've been calling and texting you all fucking night."

"What?" I ask, searching in my clutch and pulling out my burner phone. I hold it up to him. "The battery is flat. I had no idea." I turn and move over to the little table under the window and plug it in to charge. I take a quick breath to steady myself. As I straighten up, I glance out into the street, wondering if my security detail has eyes on the house.

"Fine. What happened last night?" Daryl paces back and forth between me and the door. The knife in his hand is small, but it's still a damn knife. I stand with my back to the window and place my palm against it, fingers pointing down. An odd thing to do. I hope the right person sees and understands what it means.

"What do you mean? I got the drive back and passed it to you. I left not long after you did."

He stops pacing and glares at me, his dark eyes narrow.

"It was blank. The drive was blank."

"What?" I try to sound surprised. "How can that be? The file was on it. I'm certain."

"How did you get it back off Sainz? You went back upstairs with Blythe all over you and came back down with Sainz making eyes at you."

I tilt my head and glower at him. "Don't play innocent, Daryl. I used the tools available to me to get the job done. If it was blank after you took possession of it, that's on you. Not me."

He stalks across the living room and grabs me by the throat. He hurls me around and slams me against the wall. I gasp for breath and grab at his hand but he holds me fast.

"Don't play your little games with me. You handed off a blank drive. You didn't get the data. You failed. That's on you." His breath is hot on my face. Terror grips me in a vice as tight as his hand. Tears prickle at the corners of my eyes.

He loosens his grip and instead plants his whole forearm across my chest to pin me against the wall. He raises the knife and holds it to my throat.

"Now spill. The truth. All of it. Why are you just getting home now? What happened up in those offices?"

My mind races to form a story. I raise my hands in surrender to buy time. But he doesn't loosen his hold on me.

"I knew Blythe could be manipulated, so I did. I got him to take me upstairs on the suggestion that he'd get sex. I got him to let us in to Sainz's office instead of his own. Playing drunk, I used my assets to my advantage. Men are fucking simple creatures, sometimes." I smirk and he relaxes a fraction. Enough for me to slip a hand between us and run it softly up his chest. What was I just saying? "While they were distracted, I lifted the pendant from Sainz's desk—it was just lying there—and led them both on. I thought about actually letting them spit roast me, but I didn't really want to have to go that far. We were drinking and Blythe passed out on the couch. I had to get out of there, so made an excuse and Sainz escorted me back down to the party. Right after I handed the drive to you, I left. I went to a bar to unwind. I ended up going home with the bartender. A sexy twenty two year old called Lance, or Bruce, or something. Anyway, we spent about four hours fucking, then I slept a little, then I came home to find you here. Sainz must have already wiped the drive before I swiped it back. But in any case, I'm burned now. He knows I stole data, or tried to. I'll lose my job."

Daryl releases me and steps backwards, a snarl on his lips. "Fuck."

"Exactly." I bring a hand to my chest and hold my own throat. My heart is still going crazy, but I suspect the immediate danger has passed. "If DUSK still wants that data, they'll have to find another way to get it. Leave me and my family alone. I tried. I did everything I could. I'm out of a job now, so you owe me."

He moves closer, his eyes narrowed, like he's assessing me. But he stops short of touching me and spins away, pacing in front of the door again.

He doesn't quite believe me.

"Thinking about it," I say, tapping my chin with a finger. "Sainz isn't an idiot. He must have known why I'd shown up in his office with Blythe. But he let me play my game and let me leave without calling security on me. He let me go because he knew he'd already wiped the drive and that I wasn't stealing anything. Hmm. I should have realised that. The champagne must have gone to my head more than I thought."

Daryl stops pacing and looks at me, his mouth twitching.

"He must be soft on you. Maybe we can use that."

"What are you thinking?" I ask, perching on the arm of the sofa.

"He might not sack you. Like you said, he didn't call security."

"Yeah, but not turning me in is a far cry from letting me keep my job when he knows I tried to steal data."

"Dammit. We'll have to see what happens on Monday."

"I'm not back in the office until after New Year now. My whole department is closed."

"But the building is open, right? You could try to get in, on the guise of needing to fetch something from your desk."

"I could..." I wait for him to come up with something else. But he just watches me expectantly. "Look. I did what you asked. I did everything. I went above and beyond. I let that creep Blythe grope me and stick his tongue down my throat. I'm coming right back around to you guys owing me. Big time."

"My neck's on the line here. They're pissed off as hell."

"That's really not my problem. Sorry. I need you to leave now. Tell them to stop harassing me and my parents." I get to my feet and to his credit, he backs towards the door without objection. His hand lands on the handle and he stops, looking me up and down again.

"Keep that phone on once it's charged. Don't expect it to be over yet." He swings the door open and stalks out, leaving it hanging open.

I cross to it and slam it shut. I slide the chain across as well as the deadbolt. I stand with my palms on the door, shaking all over. Fuck.

CHAPTER TWELVE

Finally, after several calming breaths, I kick off my shoes and limp to the bathroom. It's all catching up with me. My heart won't stop pounding and my hands keep shaking. I turn on the shower and the boiler groans loudly in the corner. The familiar banging from inside the ancient pipes accompanies the feeble water pressure. I strip off and step under the hot steam, wishing it was more substantial.

Tears begin to fall and I plant my hands on the tiles. The water splashes against the back of my head and my hair hangs limply on either side of my face. My shoulders shake and great sobs burst from my chest. I stay like that until the hot water runs out. Even once it goes cold, I can't move. But I scrape the snot from my face and turn my face up into the icy spray. The cold water is refreshing and rinses away the overwhelming emotions.

Eventually, I climb out of the shower and pat

myself dry with a fluffy towel. I wrap it around me and head into the bedroom, still towel drying my poker-straight hair. I lower the towel from my face and nearly jump right out of my skin.

Nicolas is standing by the old, sealed up fireplace in my bedroom.

"Fuck!" I say, half laughing. "How did you get in here?"

"I came down the chimney." There's no humour in his voice. He moves towards me, scowling. "What happened?"

"Daryl was waiting for me when I got home. He threatened me, wanted to know what happened last night. I fed him a story. He left."

"Are you alright?"

I nod. "Fine."

"Gavin's in the living room sweeping for surveillance tech. He already did in here."

"Oh." I nod. "How did you really get in? I bolted the door."

"Window," he says, jerking his head towards the bedroom window. There's a fire escape snaking up that side of the building.

"Oh."

"We'll get you a security upgrade. Your windows should have locks and your door needs an upgrade."

"Please don't go to any trouble for this rat trap."

"It's not that bad." He glances around. I have real wood floors, even though they're slightly bowed. Sash windows that my landlord claims are the originals. The plumbing may be shit and the walls paper thin, but it's clean and mostly tidy. The neighbourhood isn't too bad for north London. So maybe he's right. I shrug.

There's a short rap on the bedroom door and my head swivels towards it as Nicolas opens it. A rounded face peers through the gap, Gavin, I presume.

"All clear, Nick."

"Thanks, Gavin." Yep. "I'll see you out. But can you come back tomorrow with those upgrades we talked about?"

"Sure thing." Gavin turns towards me with a smile, sees that I'm just in a towel and hastily exits without a word. Nicolas follows him and the door chain clinks, the bolt clicks and the door opens and closes while I stand there dripping slightly on my wooden floor.

Nicolas returns and closes the bedroom door.

"I don't like it."

"You said it wasn't that bad," I reply, offended, despite my own criticism of the flat.

"Not your home. This whole situation. I don't like it."

"Oh." I sit down on the edge of the bed and hold my towel up, tucking it more firmly in on itself. "No, me neither. It's not over. I demanded DUSK release me, but Daryl didn't seem to think that was an option. I'm no use to them now. As far as they know, you're about to sack me for trying to steal from your company." I catch his eye as he stands by the door.

He moves closer, towering over me.

"Not going to happen. You still have your job."

"Thank you, but if they discover that, they'll either know you're helping me, or they'll still want me to work for them."

"Do you want me to fire you?" He cocks an eyebrow.

"Not especially, no." I look up at him. Fuck, he's hot. Even in jeans and a red t-shirt, rather than one of his fancy suits.

He reaches out and gently wipes a trickle of water from my cheek.

"You were crying. In the shower. I didn't mean to eavesdrop, I'm sorry."

I lean into his gentle touch and close my eyes.

"It's been a really difficult couple of days."

"Holly—"

The sound of my name on his tongue makes my skin tingle.

"I should leave you to get some rest," he says, low, reluctant.

"Don't." I reach for his hand as he begins to move away. "I need you."

I didn't know how true that was until the words leave my lips. I pull his hand back to my face and rest my cheek in it. I look up at him through my long lashes.

With his other hand, he reaches into his back pocket, takes out his wallet and drops it on my bedside table. His phone follows it.

I unfasten his jeans and tug them down over his hips. The bulge in his boxers begins to grow.

Nicolas withdraws his hand and yanks his t-shirt up over his head, tossing it to the floor, then kicks off his shoes and jeans.

"Are you sure?" he asks, still looking down at me with those cool, grey eyes.

"Yes, I'm sure. I need to be touched, savoured."

He drops his boxers and his cock stiffens right in front of me. I shuffle forwards and open my mouth. But he shakes his head and bends over, kissing my lips instead. His hands untuck my towel and he lets it fall before dropping onto his knees between my thighs. His fingers run down my neck and over my hard nipples. He cups one breast in a firm hand, while circling the other nipple with his thumb.

I gasp, a shiver runs through me. My head tips back.

He kisses his way down over my collar bone and lowers himself to take my left nipple into his mouth. He tugs firmly on it with his teeth, while his fingers pinch at my right nipple. His other hand runs down my side and onto my thigh. I spread wider for him and he eases a finger inside my wet pussy. His tongue flicks over my nipple and a moan bursts from my throat.

God, I need this. I need him. My skin burns and my heart beats a samba in my chest.

He pulls back and looks me in the eye. His finger slowly massaging inside me.

"What do you need right now? Slow, sensual, controlled? Or a wild fuck with no holes barred?" His voice is thick with desire.

I groan and close my eyes. His finger is still working me expertly and I'm already pretty close to coming.

"I don't know. I can't make decisions right now." Words tumble from my mouth as I wrestle them into shape. "Do what you want with me."

"Anything?"

"Anything." I moan again as my pleasure builds. "Use me."

"Never," he whispers. "I don't do that."

He picks up the pace with his finger and his thumb gets to work on my clit.

"Fuck," I cry out. I can't stay upright any longer. I drop backwards, my damp hair splays out around my head, my knees spread wide and my toes press into the floor even as my heels come up. My moans grow louder as he pushes me closer to the edge with just one finger and thumb. Damn, he's good.

"On your knees," he commands, pulling his finger out of me. "In the middle of the bed."

I whimper but do as I'm told, shuffling over and turning over onto all fours. I glance sideways and watch him open a condom packet and slide the rubber over his rock hard cock.

"You don't have to use that," I say, my breathing laboured. "I'm on birth control."

"I do have to. Much as I would love not to, I can't take any chances with you. Or anyone else."

I grumble faintly to myself. I know how smooth the skin of his dick is from when I sucked him off in the lift and I'm longing to feel it inside my pussy. But he's right.

Pregnancy isn't the only risk.

He crawls onto the bed behind me, takes hold of my hips and slowly eases his cock into my dripping wet cunt.

A low moan rumbles from my open mouth and I hang my head as I stretch for him. "Fuck," I whimper. "You're so fucking big."

He chuckles and his fingers tighten on my hips.

"Yes, I am. I love how tight you are around me. It feels so good."

I groan again as he begins to move in me. My whole body rocks gently in time with his thrusts, which are long and slow.

He moves his right hand onto the small of my back and presses me into a low dip. "That's it. Good girl."

His hips thrust harder, faster. My body rocks against him and pressure builds deep in my stomach. There's no containing it. The cry that bursts from my throat is deep, guttural, primal. The crescendo of ecstasy is overwhelming. All of the heightened emotions of the last twenty-four hours come crashing over me. My shaking arms give way and my shoulders crash onto the bed. I turn my head sideways and release a long, low moan as he fucks me even harder. The pounding is relentless. Another wave of orgasm crashes into me and I scrunch the duvet in both fists.

Nicolas grips my hips hard. I'll probably bruise. But fuck, this is the hottest sex of my life. It's raw, honest.

I cry my way through another orgasm and turn my face into the bedding so that the thick duvet swallows my scream. Tears prickle at the corners of my eyes and I let them come. A swell of emotion threatens to overwhelm me but I channel it into the pleasure I feel.

His thrusts slow, the brutal pumping morphs into long, deep strokes and I'm able to ride the wave back down from my climax. He slowly pulls out of me and I lift my head, looking back at him over my shoulder.

"Don't worry. I'm no where near done." He cracks a smile before using his thumbs to spread my cheeks.

I gasp as he presses the head of his cock against my anus. I push back up on my hands, arch my back so that my belly is as low as possible and relax my tight muscles for him. This is not my first anal rodeo.

"That's my good girl. I'm so proud that you know what to do." He eases slowly into me, one careful inch at a time.

I take long, slow breaths. I drop my head and extend the arch.

Another inch. And another. Careful, considerate. Until finally, he's buried to the fucking hilt. I never knew I could take that much. I've never felt so full in my life. I make myself keep breathing, even though I want to hold it. My sphincter pushes back, objecting to the intrusion but his soft hands caress my back and buttocks.

"Fuck. I can feel you squeezing me. It feels amazing."

"Tell me about it," I say with a laugh. "Be really careful, won't you? It's been a little while since anyone fucked my arsehole. And you're considerably bigger than him."

"I promise." He begins to pull back, just a touch, then eases back in. He goes slowly, gradually increasing the depth of his steady strokes.

"Oh God," I whimper. "That's so good."

Nicolas picks up the pace. His hands hold my hips still as he drives his cock home again. And again. And again.

My whimpers turn to cries with every thrust—short, sharp, high-pitched. The wave builds in my core again, tightening my abs and my pelvic floor. I throw my head back as the pressure becomes too much and release a cry so loud that it probably causes everyone in the street outside to look up at my window. I don't fucking care. I come hard. My pussy clenches around air.

Nicolas's cock swells inside me. I feel every movement. His breathing is ragged and broken, his thrusts become erratic.

"Fuck, yes. That's so fucking good." His voice is more like a growl. "Good girl. Such a good. Fucking. Girl." He punctuates his words with hard thrusts and comes with a growl. His cock throbs inside my arse and he holds me up, despite how much I want to collapse.

I'm a whimpering mess as he slides slowly out of me and as soon as I can, I drop down onto my face. He lays down next to me and caresses my back. Every touch sends an aftershock through my whole body.

"Feeling better?" he asks, genuine concern in his tone. I turn my face towards him and grin lopsidedly.

"Much. That was incredible. Thank you for seeing to me so thoroughly."

"I would say that the pleasure was all mine, but I'm very confident it was yours too." He leans in and kisses my lips with such tenderness it brings another tear to my eye. I kiss him back and roll onto my side. I could go again right now, honestly. I could have sex with him twenty-four seven. I wrap an arm around him and he pulls me against his body, kissing me deeply.

Eventually, we come up for air and I gaze into his eyes.

"I know it's fucking cheesy and awful, but I have to say it..." I wince as I gear up to it, but I say the words. "All I want for Christmas, is you."

He chuckles and tucks my head in under his chin. "I feel exactly the same."

CHAPTER THIRTEEN

I must have slept, because the next thing I know, the room is lit by my fairy lights, which come on on a timer at four. I'm still wrapped in Nicolas's arms, my head tucked under his chin. His hands gently caress my back and hip and when I stir, he kisses the top of my head.

"What time is it?" I ask, my voice a small croak.

"Nearly five. You needed to sleep. I think I dozed as well, to be honest. I was up twelve hours ago."

"Ugh. Why?"

"Habit. I'm an early riser."

"Hmm," I nuzzle sleepily against his chest. "What did you do before I got up?"

"Went to the gym, had a call with Japan, picked up pastries, and let the decorators in."

"A slow start to your Saturday, then," I say, grinning.

"Very."

It takes me a second before realising he's being serious. That *was* a slow start for him. An unpleasant sensation coils around my insides. How can I ever hope to keep up with him? I'm reminded again of all the glamorous blonds in Switzerland and tug myself out of his arms.

"Everything okay?" he asks, shifting up onto his arm.

"Fine. It's just, your life is so different from mine. You accomplish so much."

"I do. But the thing is, I wasn't born into wealth. I've had to earn it and every day I'm reminded that I have to fight hard to stay in the race."

"You inherited the company though," I say, propping myself up on my elbows. "Wasn't your family rich?"

"No," he shakes his head. "Asset rich, maybe. Dad built this business, sure, but he got into debt to do it and the stress nearly killed him. When I took over, I had a lot to do to make the company what it is today."

"I didn't realise." I look at him with fresh eyes. "So it hasn't always been skiing trips and supermodels."

He tilts his head and looks at me quizzically. "What do you think I was doing in St. Mortiz?"

Heat rises in my cheeks. "Oh you know, sipping Martinis in front of fires, surrounded by leggy blondes."

"I was there on business." He grins. "There was very little pleasure. And she was a brunette, not a blonde."

I gawk at him until he gives me a playful shove and

releases a chuckle.

"Whatever," I say, stifling a laugh. "It would be none of my business anyway. You're a free agent and we hadn't met yet." It's strange to think we actually met properly less than twenty four hours ago. It feels so natural, so easy, like we've been together for months, or years even.

He looks at me with such earnest eyes and I wonder if he's thinking the same thing.

"Am I a free agent?" he asks.

"I don't know. Are you?"

"What if I don't want to be?"

My breath hitches.

"Look," he shifts his weight and places a hand on my waist. "I'm not a casual hook-up kind of guy. I like being in relationships. I like having someone special to take care of, especially if she challenges me too. Whatever this is between us, it's not something I enter into lightly."

"Oh. Okay." What is that fluttering sensation in my belly? "What's your number?" Why am I asking? Will this hurt me?

"My number?"

"You know, how many people you've slept with."

"Oh," he blinks and shifts his weight. "Well, I've had four serious relationships. And..." His eyes flit back and forth as if he's counting. "Seven more casual or short-lived relationships."

"And no one night stands?"

"No. So, eleven women."

"Huh." I couldn't have been more wrong about him. I'd assumed he was a bit of a playboy, just very good at keeping it out of the media. But for an attractive, wealthy man in his forties, his number is surprisingly low.

"What's yours?"

Ah. That's how this is going to hurt me. I hold my tongue and stare at the patch of bed between us.

"Come on, fair's fair," he says, playfully nudging my side.

"Yes, I suppose so. I don't want you to think less of me. I've been fairly promiscuous in my youth."

"I won't. I don't judge."

"Okay." Damn. I'm going to have to think about this. "There was my high school boyfriend. Then my boyfriend at uni. Erm..." This is going to be the hardest part. Heat rises in my cheeks. "Then I had a situationship, as the youngsters say today. Back then we called it complicated. In my third year of uni, I shared a house with a girlfriend and three guys. There was quite a lot of bed-hopping that year."

"Really?" He leans in, his tone curious.

"Yeah. We all slept together, in various combos. It was like a porn movie." I nod in mock seriousness.

"Is there video footage?"

"God, I hope not." I shake my head, trying not to remember anything too closely. "Anyway, Kirsty and I actually tried being a couple after that. We got a flat together and were vaguely monogamous for about a year."

"Vaguely?"

"We had a couple of relapse threesomes with Danny, one of the guys we'd lived with."

Nicolas rubs a hand over his face and I can't tell if he's appalled, or titillated.

"Erm, so that ended and I had a slutty phase. Honestly, I don't remember half their names, but I can recall most of their faces. My best guess is about fifteen casual things in that time."

"Men and women?"

"Yeah. Is that okay?"

"Of course. Go on."

"Then I met Theo." Okay, no, this was going to be the hardest part. "I was twenty six. We were together for three years. I thought he was the one. We lived together. Just before Christmas I found an engagement ring in his desk drawer and got very excited. I waited, thinking he was going to propose on Christmas Day. But he didn't. And just after New Year, I came home one day to find all his stuff gone. He'd moved out without a word. He changed his phone number. Just totally ghosted me."

"Fuck, sorry." His face is aghast. He touches my shoulder and I give a shrug.

"It's not your fault. About six months later, a mutual friend told me that he'd moved to Canada and had got married. It turned out," I take a deep breath and huff it out. "That he'd been seeing her for two years and it was her that he bought the ring for."

"No!"

"Yep. When I thought he was travelling for work, he was still in London, splitting his time between us. He was living with both of us."

"Fucking hell."

"Don't worry, there's a happy ending."

"Oh?"

"About a year after he left me, the other woman, Alice, reached out to me. She'd had no idea about me until the same friend who told me the truth also told her. She was divorcing him. She was very apologetic and turned out to be lovely. She did very well out of the divorce and she offered me some of the money as compensation. It wasn't a fortune, just enough to pay off my student loans and dig myself out of the financial hole he'd left me in when he moved out and left me in an apartment I couldn't afford on my own. Anyway, she and I are still good friends to this day. She moved back to London. I'm actually having drinks with her on Christmas Eve." I try to smile, but this story still hurts like hell.

"I guess that is a happy ending. So was he the last person on your list?"

"Not exactly, no. I've had three more sexual partners since him, including you. So I think that makes my total twenty five. Was I included in yours?"

"You weren't. Most remiss of me. That brings my total to twelve."

"Well doesn't that make us both the most festive couple ever?" I say, grinning and trying to shake off my regrets and sadness.

"It does." He nods and his gaze scans my skin. "Thank you for sharing all of that with me, I know it can't have been easy."

I press my lips together and nod.

"Listen, I have a dinner tonight. Would you like to come?"

"What kind of dinner?"

"A work thing. The last one before I get to switch off for a few days. I hate to leave you alone all night after such a raw conversation. Besides, I'd love to have your engaging company for what might otherwise be a somewhat dull event."

"Would it be, like, a date?"

"Yes, it would. In public. How do you feel about that?"

Those butterflies go fluttering through my stomach again.

"Lovely. But what about DUSK? What if they're following one or both of us and see us together?"

"We can't hide from them. We can't stop living. We'll be careful."

Nicolas glances at the dark sky beyond the window, then back at me.

"I should go. I need to go home and get ready for this dinner."

I shift onto my side. "Assuming my place is being watched, how will you get out without being seen?"

He pushes a hand through his thick hair, still mussed from sleep. "By making sure they're not looking when I leave." He picks up his phone from the bedside table, taps a quick message, and waits. "Gavin will create a distraction."

Watching him stand, still gloriously naked, makes my chest ache. But then he starts pulling his clothes together with that calm precision that's so him. By the time he's sliding his watch onto his wrist, he looks every inch the powerful, controlled man again.

"Meet me at Claridge's at eight."

Claridge's. My stomach does a nervous somersault. That's a world of glittering trees, champagne towers, and gowns worth more than my rent. I don't belong there. And yet, part of me thrills at the idea of stepping into his world, at his side.

Before I can answer, his phone buzzes. He glances at the screen and nods once, decisive.

"Good. Gavin's in position. When you hear a car alarm out front, that's my cover. I'll slip out the back way."

"Nicolas..." My voice is soft, wavering. "Just... be careful."

He crouches by the bed, cups my cheek in his warm hand, and places a sizzling kiss on my lips. "Always. And Holly—" his thumb brushes my jaw, "—wear something that makes you feel unstoppable tonight. Because that's how I want the world to see you."

My throat tightens, but I nod.

Then, as if on cue, a sharp blare of a car alarm splits the street outside, which sets of Mr Gomolka's pit bull again. Nicolas presses one last kiss to my lips—brief, grounding—and then he's moving, slipping the window open onto the fire escape with quiet efficiency.

And just like that, he's gone, swallowed by the dark.

CHAPTER FOURTEEN

I take the bus to Highbury and Islington and change for the Victoria line. I finally have time to think —and to feel the pulse of the city beneath my feet.

The tube is warm, stuffy, smelling faintly of wet coats and mince pies in paper bags. A toddler sings Jingle Bells out of tune while his mother scrolls her phone with weary thumbs. A man in a Santa hat snores gently in his seat by the doors, his shopping bags spilling onto the floor. It's ordinary, it's London, and for once I'm grateful for the anonymity.

I clutch the cold pole as the train rattles through tunnels, every lurch of the carriage making me sway. My reflection in the dark window looks like someone else— dressed up, hair smoothed into something halfway glamorous, a slash of red lipstick daring the world to underestimate me.

I get off at Oxford Circus and music echoes in the

tunnel from a busker, his battered saxophone giving "Silent Night" a bluesy lilt. I emerge from the underground station into the bustle of where Oxford Street meets Regent Street. The pavements are a crush of late-night shoppers, every shop front lit like a jewelled box. Fairy lights glitter above the street, glowing against the indigo sky. I breathe in the mingled scents of roasted chestnuts, mulled wine, and the faint whiff of horse manure from the carriages offering Christmas rides down Oxford Street.

I tug my coat tighter, heels clicking against the pavement as I make my way towards Claridge's. A choir in red robes sings "O Come, All Ye Faithful" on the corner, their voices soaring above the honks of black cabs. Coins jingle into their buckets, a child claps, and for a fleeting moment I feel like just another Londoner swept up in the season, not a woman caught in the jaws of something darker.

But then a shadow at the edge of the crowd lingers too long, and the magic tightens back into unease.

I reach the prestigious hotel five minutes late. The doorman in his dark grey livery tips his hat as he pulls the door open for me, and I step inside. The shift is immediate—London's winter chaos gives way to Claridge's hush, the air perfumed with pine, cinnamon, and champagne. Soft piano music drifts from somewhere unseen, blending with the low hum of moneyed voices.

And there, at the heart of it all, towers the Christmas tree. This year's design is a glittering confection of glass baubles and sculptural ribbons, glowing like starlight in the vast foyer. Guests cluster nearby, posing for photos, laughing too loudly in sequinned gowns and tuxedos.

But I only see him.

Nicolas stands at the base of the grand, sweeping staircase beside the tree, a dark figure cut sharp in black tie, steel-grey eyes scanning the entrance until they land on me. That look—steady, claiming—makes my breath catch. He straightens, smoothing his jacket with one hand, as though the sight of me demands precision.

I tug my burgundy coat tighter, nerves fluttering in my chest. Then I shrug it off, passing it to the waiting attendant. The black dress beneath clings in all the right places, hem grazing my thighs, devastatingly backless, and neckline daring and unapologetic. My long, red hair is tied up in an elegant top knot and fastened with a glittering black clip. My bold high heels are bright red. Cool air brushes bare skin as I walk forward, every heel-strike loud against the marble floor.

Nicolas's gaze darkens. Hunger. Pride. Possession. He doesn't hide any of it.

"Good God," he murmurs when I reach him, his voice low enough that only I can hear. His eyes trace me from head to toe, lingering just long enough to make heat coil in my belly. "You'll make the tree look underdressed."

"Stop," I whisper, cheeks flushing. He places a tender hand on the small of my back, his manicured hand soft on my bare skin, and leans in to brush a kiss against my cheek. It's dangerously intimate in this rather public place.

"I will never stop." He offers me his arm, formal, old-fashioned, and achingly sexy. When I place my hand on it, he leans closer, lips brushing the shell of my ear. "Every man in this foyer is wishing he were me right now. Let them look. You're mine."

My knees wobble, but I manage a smile. Together we turn toward the grand staircase, where a discreet sign indicates the private dining suites. Staff hold the doors for us, perfectly polite, as though they haven't just seen me melt into Nicolas Sainz like butter left too close to the fire.

The corridors of the hotel are lined with thick carpet and soft lighting guides our way. Nicolas shows me into a private dining room of dusty pink curtains and comfortable chairs around an immaculately-laid table. It's a fairly small room, perfect for a private gathering. Most of the seats at the table are already occupied and every eye turns to us as we enter.

"Good evening, everyone," Nicolas says we enter. He is unhurried, used to people waiting for him. A ripple of greetings runs around the dozen or so people present. Older men in suits, a few wives in their best jewellery, and a few women without dates—all dressed in professional and formal attire—look expectantly in our direction. "May I introduce Holly Harrington, a rising star at Ostoria."

Polite nods and smiles bounce back at me. No one is fooled. Including me. I'm here because I look good on his arm. I'm okay with that. Mostly.

Nicolas slides a chair out for me and slides it back in beneath me as I sit. I try to recall the valuable lessons

I learned from Julia Roberts in a strikingly similar situation to this as I look down at all the silverware on the table. Nicolas takes his seat next to me and a waiter promptly leans past me to fill a glass with water. I glance along the table and see that everyone has water, there's no alcohol yet. I look up at the waiter when he finishes pouring and give him a nod of thanks.

Nicolas leans close, his hand on my thigh under the table. "You okay? You look shell-shocked." He keeps his voice low enough for only me to hear him.

I press my lips together and nod. "Fine."

Another couple arrives and are greeted by everyone else. They take their seats opposite me and Nicolas. With a subtle nod from Nicolas to indicate that everyone has arrived, the wait staff file out of the room.

The woman next to me turns to me and greets me with a warm smile. She's silver-haired and also dressed in black—all sequins and modesty though, unlike my little black dress.

"Hello," she says, her voice warm. "Holly, is it?"

"That's right." I reply, taking her offered hand.

"Meredith Ford," she says. Her handshake is firm. "I'm glad to see Nicolas with a nice young lady, for a change."

I crack a smile. "I'm very happy to accompany him. It's a beautiful venue."

"It is. You know, my husband and I spent our wedding night here fifty two years ago."

"Oh, how lovely." I peer past her to the man on her other side.

She chuckles. "That's not him. He's in Florida."

"Oh, my apologies."

"No need, dear. Golf has rather more allure for him these days than board rooms and business dinners."

"I suppose that's fair enough." Before I can ask her in what capacity she's at this function, the sommelier in his dark grey and gold uniform arrives with an open bottle. He stands beside Nicolas and pours a little wine into his glass. I watch in awe as Nicolas tastes it, thinks for a moment and gives a small nod. The sommelier slips out without a word. There isn't so much as a ripple in the gentle babble of conversation around the table.

A moment later, the wait staff file back in with more bottles of the same wine and begin pouring it.

"It's a Sancerre Sauvignon Blanc from the Loire Valley," Nicolas says softly at my ear.

"Now you're just showing off." I grin at him and he smiles back.

As soon as the wine is poured, the wait staff are back with the appetiser. I'm momentarily surprised, as I didn't order yet, but when I glance up and down the table, I notice the lack of menus. I lean over to Nicolas and whisper just for him.

"Is it a fixed menu?"

"It is," he replies softly, his hand squeezing my thigh. "I hope you enjoy everything. You're not vegetarian, are you?"

I shake my head as a plate is placed in front of me. I blink down at the food, unsure what it is.

"Help me out," I say out of the corner of my mouth.

Nicolas leans close again, his breath is warm on my neck. "Seared scallops, with cauliflower purée, crispy pancetta, and a drizzle of truffle oil."

"Oh, sure. I knew that." I turn and kiss him lightly on the cheek. He grins and lets go of my leg to pick up his cutlery. I check which set he takes and copy him just as he gets into conversation with the man opposite him.

The rest of the meal passes in a flurry of shop-talk, some gossip, and so much delicious and rich food that I feel fit to burst by the end. The main course is venison with a silky Burgundy Pinot Noir. Dessert is the highlight though. A traditional Christmas pudding soufflé with brandy crème Anglaise.

I feel both utterly out of my depth, and also completely safe with Nicolas by my side, helping me to navigate this strange, moneyed world.

As coffee is served, I prop my elbow on the table, not caring if it's uncouth, and cross my long legs towards him so that my foot can rub up his shin.

"So, have you ever stayed overnight here?" I ask.

"There hasn't been a great need to stay in any London hotels, given that I live here," he says, a small smile playing over his lips. "But yes. I have stayed here once. Was that a subtle hint that you want to get a room?"

His voice is low, but it's a small gathering and I'm sure we're being overheard. Still, I press a little closer. "It might be nice."

There's no chance I could ever afford to stay at a hotel like this. Why not take advantage of the opportunity? But I'm not going to say that out loud in this company.

Nicolas's eyes narrow slightly as he scans my face and neckline. I rub my foot higher up his leg. With a sharp intake of breath, he turns and indicates to a staff member behind him. The young man in his starched uniform steps forward and bends slightly.

"Would you see if there's a suite available for us for tonight, please?" He slips the young man some cash and he gives Nicolas a nod before hurrying from the room.

The conversation at the table carries on, a polite murmur of voices over the clink of cutlery and fine china. I sip the last of my coffee, its bitterness cutting through the richness of the meal, and let my hand rest lightly on Nicolas's thigh under the table. He covers it with his own, anchoring me.

A discreet cough draws our attention. The young waiter who took Nicolas's request leans in between us, his voice pitched low. "The Mayfair Terrace Suite is available, sir. Everything is being prepared now."

"Perfect," Nicolas replies smoothly. He glances around the table and gives a faint incline of his head. "It's been a pleasure, as always. But if you'll excuse us, Holly and I have another engagement."

There are murmured goodbyes, polite smiles, knowing glances. Meredith squeezes my hand as I rise, her eyes warm with amusement. I don't even want to think what she suspects.

The staff swoop in, clearing plates as though we were never there.

Nicolas shakes everyone's hands and does his dutiful goodbyes as the guests all file out. Once it's just us and the staff remaining, he turns me gently to face him, and with that commanding calm of his says, "Give us the room, please."

The maître d' bows his head, understanding, and gestures for the last of the staff to slip quietly away.

When the door clicks shut behind them, silence falls. Just us. The scent of pine from the decorations lingers in the air, mingling with brandy and coffee.

Nicolas steps closer, his eyes dark, hungry. He presses himself against me, his arousal evident.

"Hmm. Hadn't we better get to that suite?" I ask.

"Soon. I want you here first."

I glance over his shoulder towards the door, but we're quite alone.

"There's something else I want to eat," he says, his voice thick and low. "And I was raised to always eat at the table."

I draw my lower lip between my teeth as he backs me up against the table. I sit on the edge of it, the thick tablecloth bunching slightly under me as I slide onto it.

Nicolas lifts the hem of my skirt and tucks his fingers into the sides of my lace thong. He tugs the flimsy fabric down and discards the garment onto the floor. He cups my face in his hands and kisses me, deep, slow, and sensual. We feast on each other, as if we hadn't just eaten a filling, gourmet meal.

Finally, he pulls back and drops slowly to his knees, pushing my dress up past my hips and spreading my legs wide on either side of him. I gasp as his fingers slide into me. I drop my hands onto the table behind me and brace myself. A glass topples over and rolls away from my fingers, but I don't care enough to stop it. His tongue is already on my clit.

My eyes flutter closed and a soft moan escapes my mouth.

Nicolas works his two fingers deeper, pressing against my g-spot, while his tongue circles my clit in precise movements. He murmurs against my pussy, his hot breath making me even wetter. The groan that rumbles out from my chest will be clearly audible from the other side of the door. I gasp and silence myself. Holding in the noises I want to make is harder than I care to admit. But Nicolas is relentless and is pushing me swiftly towards climax.

My head drops back so I'm looking straight up at the ceiling. My thighs clench and my throat aches from holding back.

Nicolas pauses and chuckles softly.

"You're being so quiet. Such a good girl. But you don't have to hold back. I want you to come so hard they hear you in the street outside."

"I can't do that," I gasp, fighting for breath.

"Yes you can, beautiful." He dips back between my thighs and resumes his second dessert. His fingers move swiftly inside me and his tongue flicks harder and faster, pushing me towards the cliff-edge.

"No," I groan, still fighting it. "Oh God."

"Come for me, sweetheart," he says against my throbbing pussy.

"Fuck!" I scream at the top of my lungs, unable to

fight it any more. My inner walls clamp down on his fingers and a gush of fluid spills out of me onto the cream table cloth. "Fuck yes! Don't stop!" I collapse onto my back on top of napkins, unused cutlery and some decorative holly. A massive wave of pleasure surges through me, shaking me from head to toe. One of my shoes drops to the floor with a heavy thud.

Nicolas continues to stroke, suck and lick even as I writhe like a demon is resisting exorcism from my body. He holds me firmly with his other hand as he makes me come again. And again.

After multiple intense waves, I go limp. My clit throbs painfully and I'm certain I can't possibly come any more. I clench my thighs together and push his head away from me with a feeble hand. He stops immediately and slowly rubs my thighs with both hands.

"Are you alright?" he asks, his voice heavy.

"Uh-huh," I reply, waving a hand.

He chuckles and takes hold of both of my hands, pulling me up to sitting and clasping my back to hold me up.

"Did you enjoy that?"

"What do you think?" I ask, smirking and flopping against his body.

"I'm not sure. I had a limited view down there. You could have been more vocal." There's a playful tone in his voice and I fix him with a mock scowl.

"I don't know how I'm going to show my face out there now." I cover my face with my hands. He gently removes them.

"You walk tall. You walk like you own this place and can do what you like here."

"That's what you do."

"Yes."

"Because you could actually buy this hotel if you wanted. I don't have that power, or authority."

"But no one knows that," he says, bumping his nose against mine. His lips press against mine, firm but tender. He tastes salty from me. When our lips part, he winks and reaches for my fallen shoe. He gently replaces it on my foot and helps me down from the table.

I scoop, unsteadily on my three inch heels, to pick up my knickers, and stuff them into my small, black velvet bag.

"Right," I say. "Take me to this magnificent suite and do that to me again and I'll bring the fucking house down."

Nicolas takes my hand and leads me out into the corridor. There's not a soul in sight, much to my relief. We head towards the foyer, but he stops at a carpeted staircase up and turns to face me.

"Wait here a moment. I need to speak to the concierge. I'll be right back."

I nod, slightly light-headed still and glad not to have to cross the marble foyer on such shaky feet. I'd be like Bambi. Not good. I'm tucked slightly out of sight and lean against the wall, my clutch tucked under one arm.

Movement to my left catches my eye and walking towards me are two members of staff. One big, broad man in the doorman's livery, the other is the waiter who arranged our suite for us. I smile towards him, but his features are stony. I try not to think about what he must think of me. Of me with Nicolas. Of why we wanted a suite. I look at my feet as the men draw closer. Disquiet filling my veins.

As they draw level with me, the big doorman grabs me and yanks me away from the wall. I try to cry out, but his hand is over my mouth before I can make a sound. My wide eyes fix on the white-jacketed waiter, who lunges at me with a syringe. A sharp prick pierces my neck. The Christmas lights blur. The faint notes of the lobby piano seem to echo from far, far away. I thrash my legs, but my arms are pinned; after a few seconds, all the fight drains out of me. My clutch hits the carpet with a soft thud as my body goes limp. I'm scooped up onto his shoulder—tree lights spinning overhead, the carols fading—and then everything goes black.

CHAPTER FIFTEEN

Cold air kisses my bare legs. The rest of me is on fire—the kind of heat that comes from fear you can't shake off.

My head throbs as consciousness drags me upright. The air smells of metal and bleach. A single strip light hums overhead, flickering now and then like it can't quite commit to staying on. My wrists are zip-tied behind the back of a metal chair, ankles bound too. My head throbs; the sedative's dull edge lingers like the aftertaste of bad wine.

A low creak draws my attention to the door. Daryl stands there, arms crossed, looking everywhere but at me.

The lock clicks and the door opens.

"Good evening, Holly."

The woman's voice is smooth, assured—like a glass of whisky poured over ice. She glides into the room in a tailored navy suit and heels that whisper across the concrete floor. Mid-forties, sleek dark hair in a chignon, expensive watch, cool smile. The kind of woman who could have been my HR director in another life.

"I'm Dawn." She lowers herself gracefully into the opposite chair. "You've caused us quite a headache."

My throat is dry, but I find my voice. "Sorry about that. I'll send an aspirin."

A smile ghosts across her lips. "Humour under pressure. I like that. It's a good sign—means you haven't given up yet."

"I didn't realise that was an option."

"It always is. But I don't think you're the giving-up type." She smiles faintly. "I can see why Daryl likes you. Sharp tongue. Sharp mind." She cants her head and studies me. "We don't have to be enemies, you know. I'd much prefer a conversation."

"About what?"

She lifts her eyes. "The flash drive. The one you handed over last night."

I stare at her blankly. "What about it?"

"It was empty." Her tone doesn't sharpen, doesn't even rise. That's somehow worse. "I want to know if you knew that when you gave it to Daryl."

I swallow. "Of course not."

"I want to believe you." Dawn folds her hands on the table. "But you were alone with Nicolas Sainz before the hand off. He had the opportunity to alter it—or to convince you to. So I'll ask again, and I want you to take a moment before you answer: did you know it was blank?"

"I didn't." My voice comes out steadier than I expect. "Why would I risk my parents for something like that?"

"Because maybe you thought Sainz could protect you. Maybe he promised he would. Maybe you thought you could play both sides."

I let out a small, incredulous laugh. "That's quite a story."

"Isn't it? And yet here we are."

Daryl shifts by the door, chewing his thumbnail and eyeing me warily. Dawn lifts one manicured finger and he stills, like a dog trained to heel. Then her gaze slides back to me—warm, almost maternal, which somehow makes it worse.

"You've been through a lot these last few days," she says. "I can only imagine how frightening it's been. The secrecy, the lies, that charming boss of yours." She tilts her head, studying me. "You must have been very convincing to get that close to him."

"I'm just good at my job," I say carefully.

"Oh, I don't doubt it." She leans forward, elbows on the table, perfume soft and expensive. "That's why I'm here. I don't want to hurt you, Holly. I want to help you find a way out of this mess."

"By working for you again?"

"Possibly." She smiles but it's about as warm as a shark. "I'm sure Sainz wiped that drive. I just don't know if you were complicit, or collateral. Help me understand which."

"Help you?" I lean forward as far as my restraints allow. "You threatened my parents, you had me drugged and dragged here, and you want my help?"

Her smile doesn't falter. "You'd be surprised how much people are willing to share when they feel understood. So let's make this simple. You tell me what Sainz said or did last night, and I'll make sure this doesn't go any further. You and your parents can go back to your little life. No more surveillance, no more visits to your homes."

My pulse spikes, but I manage a small, humourless smile. "You think you can fix this with a bit of charm?"

"I don't need charm," she says softly. "I have leverage."

For a moment, the only sound is the hum of the light and the faint tap of her manicured nails against the table.

Then I exhale slowly and fix her with what I hope passes for a weary, reluctant look. "You just want to know what happened in his office last night?"

"That's all."

"Alright," I say, lowering my voice, leaning forward as if confiding something dangerous. "And if I tell you, you'll let me go?"

Dawn's smile deepens. "If you tell me the truth."

I nod slowly, giving her exactly what she wants—apparent surrender. "Fine. But you'll want to keep an eye on Daryl for this part."

Dawn glances over her shoulder at him. He looks startled. I seize the moment—the flicker of power between them.

"Unless," I add, voice barely above a whisper, "you're one hundred percent sure it wasn't him that wiped the drive."

The silence that follows could slice through glass.

Dawn's expression doesn't flicker, but the faintest pulse ticks at her temple. She turns to glance at Daryl, then back at me, her voice still honey-smooth. "I'm sure."

Daryl stiffens. "She's bluffing. We already know Sainz wiped it clean."

I tilt my head. "Are you sure Daryl didn't replace it? Because Nicolas Sainz doesn't do anything halfway. If he knew I was working with you, he wouldn't have let me walk out of there. Not without a security escort and immediate revocation of my access."

Dawn leans back and fixes me with an appraising stare. "You're good." She rolls her tongue over her teeth beneath her glossy lips.

"To the best of my knowledge, the data was right where I put it. It passed through Daryl's hands before getting to your people. That's all I'm saying."

Daryl's nostrils flare. "You bitch—"

"Enough." Dawn's voice cracks like a whip. She doesn't raise it, but the force behind it stills him mid-step.

He hesitates, fists flexing. But he backs down.

Dawn turns back to me, her poise recovered. "You're smart. I'll give you that."

"Maybe," I murmur, "or maybe I'm just tired of

being everyone's pawn."

"Then stop playing games." Her tone sharpens just slightly. "Tell me exactly what Sainz said to you before you left the office that night. You got the drive back off him, whether it was blank or not at that point is almost irrelevant. Reassure me that he didn't turn you."

"We didn't even talk about the drive." I heave a sigh. "I already told Daryl what happened. I used Blythe to get upstairs. We went into Sainz's office and he was there. We drank. I flirted with them, led them on. I lifted the drive without him noticing and I left. I don't see what's so hard to understand about that. If he wiped the drive, he did it before I got up there. But like I said, if he'd looked at that drive and seen what I'd stolen, he wouldn't have let me walk out of there. I think you know that. I think this is all just a performance. Because the man you really want is right behind you." I jerk my head in Daryl's direction.

That lands. Dawn's eyes flicker—tiny, almost imperceptible—but it's there. She glances at Daryl again and the fissure in their trust splits wide open.

Daryl lurches towards me. "She's playing you, same as she played Sainz! You weren't even there, Dawn. You don't know what she's capable of—"

"Neither do you," I cut in quietly.

He rounds on me, furious. And that's when I do it.

The second he steps too close, I head butt him hard, right in the face. A loud crack and a gush of blood announce the break in his nose and he reels backwards, clutching his face and groaning.

"Stop!" Dawn snaps, standing fast. But Daryl is

incensed. He lunges at me again, blood pouring down his chin. All she can do is stagger backwards out of the way.

I jerk sideways, straining against the zip ties. They bite painfully into my wrists and ankles. Daryl knocks me and the chair over and a cry bursts from me as I land hard on the concrete floor, the chair crushing my arms. Agony sears up my arms and through my head.

The door clangs open, slamming back against the wall and between Daryl's legs I glimpse a small army filing into the room. A figure clad all in black forces Dawn against a wall and another pair of men in combat boots drag Daryl away from me, thrashing wildly.

Confusion swells, fogging my mind and my gaze darts around the room. Softer hands are on me then and a man squats in front of me, swiping a balaclava from his face. Nicolas.

Tears spill down my cheeks and loud sobs burst from my trembling lips.

Someone cuts my zip ties and Nicolas's lips are moving but I can't hear a word he's saying between my own sobs, Daryl's shouts, and the voices of the security team. Nicolas scoops me up into his strong arms and clutches me against his chest. The calming scent of his cologne cuts through the metallic tang of the basement.

"You didn't think Halcyon weren't tracking Miss Harrington's every step, did you, Dawn?" Someone asks. "You should know better."

I don't fully comprehend what's happening as I'm ushered from the room surrounded by big men in Kevlar. Nicolas stays behind and I glance over my shoulder just in time to see him walking slowly towards Dawn, thunder in his eyes, before the heavy metal door swings shut.

CHAPTER SIXTEEN

Someone sits me down in the open back door of a black van, wraps a blanket around my shoulders and starts to check me for injuries. Besides feeling sore, I don't seem to be hurt. The night air bites at my bare legs, but the blanket smells of clean wool and diesel, which is oddly comforting.

The flashing, orange, hazard lights of unmarked vehicles bounce off the warehouse walls. Men and women in dark tactical gear move with quiet efficiency, voices low over comms. One of them shines a small torch in my eyes and asks me to follow his finger. I do. My head throbs but I manage a nod when he asks if I'm alright.

A woman nearby talks hurriedly on her phone. I just catch my parents' names in her rushed conversation. When her call ends, she turns to a familiar face, Gavin, and relays something that I can't make out, but my gaze is locked on the pair of them.

Gavin nods and his head swivels in my direction. He dismisses her and heads my way.

"Miss Harrington, your parents are safe and secure. They have no idea what's happened. May I suggest it remain that way?"

I nod, still numb, but relief begins to warm my extremities.

Then, through the blur, I see him.

Nicolas steps out of the building, jacket gone, shirt sleeves rolled, a shadow of fury still etched into the hard lines of his face. The moment his gaze finds me, the tension breaks. He crosses the distance in long, sure strides.

"Holly." His voice cracks on my name. He halts in front of me and his hands hover for a second before they touch—checking, reassuring. "You're safe. It's over."

I nod, though my throat is too tight for words. My fingers curl into the fabric of his shirt. He folds me against his chest, and the world narrows to his warmth, his heartbeat steady against my ear.

"Let's take you home," he murmurs. He scoops me into his arms and carries me to his car, my bare feet swinging gently. My shoes are lost somewhere.

The car ride passes in a blur of street lights and city shadows. I drift in and out of consciousness until we arrive at his building. He keeps a secure hold on me as we ride up in the lift and when the lift doors open into his penthouse, I almost cry.

It's transformed.

Garlands twist up the staircase, fairy lights hang like a waterfall of light over the vast windows, and the enormous tree by the windows glows with golden warmth. The scent of pine and cinnamon fills the air. Candles flicker in glass jars along the mantel. It's magical—too beautiful for the night I've just survived.

Nicolas unwraps me from the blanket, every movement slow, careful. His usual confidence has softened into something almost shy.

I walk slowly into the living room, gazing in awe at the wonderland I've stepped into.

"Do you like it?"

"It's stunning." I come to a halt and our eyes meet. He's watching me with a concerned frown and a reluctant twitch at the corner of his mouth. I hold a hand out and he closes the gap between us, scooping my hand up to his lips to lay a soft kiss on the knuckles.

"So are you. You handled yourself admirably throughout all of this."

I snort and shake my head. "I don't think so."

"You handled each crisis fearlessly. If I didn't know better, I'd say you'd been training for this for years."

"Well, that's very flattering, but it doesn't feel true right now. Give me a couple of days to process it all."

"That's fair."

"What will happen now? What did you say to Dawn?"

He guides me onto the nearest sofa and sits beside me, holding both of my hands.

"The less you know, the better, but rest assured that

this nightmare is over for your whole family."

I shake my head, scowling. "No, don't do that. I've been in the thick of this, I need to know it all."

"Holly—"

"No, I mean it. Tell me everything."

"Alright. I'm buying out your parents' debt and cancelling it. Daryl and Dawn won't bother you any more."

"What does that mean?" Nerves tingle through my fingers, my pulse stutters. How far would he go?

"Just that they've been persuaded that you are not a threat to DUSK and not an asset either. They are both alive and mostly well. You broke Daryl's nose." A ghost of a smile catches his lips.

"You just handled all of this outside of the law? No police?" The nerves remain. I trust him, but I wonder exactly what he's embroiled in. I'd never given too much thought to what exactly DUSK wanted me to steal. Client data was what they told me and I took it at face value. But now?

"It's for the best. My people are very capable." He cracks a small smile.

I hold his gaze and a word bubbles up in my memory. "Nicolas, what is Halcyon?"

His face pales slightly. "A client. Can we leave it at that?"

"What did DUSK want?"

"Information on Halcyon. It was vital they didn't get it. A lot of people could have been put in harms way. I had to do whatever it took to keep those files away from DUSK."

"And they'll really just drop it now?"

"I'm very persuasive." He leans closer and cups my cheek in his warm hand. I close my eyes and melt into him. I can live with that. If he keeps touching me like this.

"I need to feel warm. I need you." I open my eyes and look into his, my cheeks warming under his touch.

"I need you too." He leans in and kisses me, slow, tender.

Warmth blooms from deep inside me, rapidly filling me with heat. My core becomes molten and I need more than this. I climb into his lap and deepen the kiss. I'm still not wearing any underwear, from when he removed it after dinner and my short dress rides up over my hips. Nicolas plants his hands on my hips and I grind against him, moaning into his mouth.

He scoops me up and deposits me on my back on the thick, white rug in front of the towering Christmas tree. Its blinking lights reflect in his eyes as he tugs off his shirt. I shimmy my dress up and tug it off over my head, leaving me naked before him. His hungry eyes feast on my smooth skin and full breasts. He unzips his trousers, his gaze not leaving my body, and removes the rest of his clothes. I watch as he puts on a condom with growing heat in his grey eyes. When he finally lowers himself onto me, I'm dripping wet and ready for him.

Nicolas eases his cock into me and I arch into him. Writhing on the floor together under the festive lights, we become one, our bodies moulding to each other. His arms cradle my shoulders, his hands caress my hair and face. His lips savour my mouth.

Every inch of me tingles and my legs lock around his hips. Slow, sensual pleasure swells inside me and when I come, it's more like a flood than an explosion. He follows swiftly, throbbing inside me and moaning softly at my ear as he climaxes.

He slows his thrusts, moving slowly in me and gazing into my eyes, a soft smile on his lips. I grin up at him and stroke his face.

"Nicolas, I have to tell you something."

"Hmm?"

"I'm developing feelings for you."

"You know, I think that might be contagious, because I'm catching feelings too." He dips his head and kisses me again, swift and soft. Then he eases out of me and collapses onto the rug beside me.

I roll onto my side and stare at this incredible man who has given me so much in such a short time. This can't be my life. What did I do to get so lucky?

We sleep finally, in his enormous bed and spend the next two days shut away in his penthouse, making love, eating and sleeping and absolutely nothing else. It's heaven.

When Christmas Eve comes around, I have my plans with Alice and reluctantly leave his side. I take the opportunity to buy him a gift—an expensive red, silk tie that I hope he'll love.

"You're glowing," Alice tells me when I arrive for drinks. "Have you gone and fallen in love?"

"Maybe," I reply, grinning. It doesn't scare me, even

though maybe the speed should.

We enjoy some festive cocktails and get all caught up—except I can't tell her any details about the last week. At midnight, nicely tipsy, I do as Nicolas instructed, and call his driver to come and collect me. I'm driven back to Chelsea and ride up in the private lift to his penthouse. When the doors open, he's waiting for me wearing nothing but a big, red bow around his neck. I burst out laughing and stumble on my high heels into his arms.

"You look festive," I say before planting a kiss on his lips.

"Merry Christmas, Holly." He scoops me into his arms and kisses me deeply. When we part, his eyes are sparkling. "Come." He takes my hand and leads me up the stairs to his room. Grinning, I follow eagerly and kick off my shoes as soon as we cross the threshold.

He undresses me slowly, leaving whispering touches on my skin. He tugs the bow from around his neck and drapes the length of fabric around mine. The thick velvet is smooth against my skin.

"When we met, you enjoyed me binding you. Has your experience the other night taken that off the table for us?"

I shake my head, suddenly finding it hard to swallow. "No, I'd still like that."

"Good." His voice is low and thick with need. He brings my wrists together at my throat and carefully ties them with the velvet, binding my arms to my chest. He leads me to the bed and helps me onto it on my front, my tied hands just free enough to elevate my head. My heart pounds and my head swims from the alcohol, but I'm quickly sobering. His quiet dominance is more intoxicating than the cocktails.

Nicolas nudges my knees apart and rotates me half onto my side. He kneels between my legs and caresses my exposed hip and thigh. I look over my shoulder, watching him as he strokes himself hard.

"Fuck. You're beautiful." His voice is a low rumble in his chest. "I could spend my whole life fucking you."

"Same," I say, my own voice little more than a rasp.

He moves over to the bedside table, takes out a condom and slips it on. He stands beside me, stroking himself again. I lie there, unable to move and pulse stuttering. Heat pooling inside my pussy. When he crawls back onto the bed at my feet, I hold my breath in anticipation. He straddles my lower leg and spreads me wide as he lowers his hips. He eases himself into me and the angle is sensational. I cry out as I take in his full length. He plants his hands on my hip and begins to thrust, slow and deep.

"Fuck!" I cry out, unable to control myself. I deepen the twist in my torso and crane my neck to look at him properly as he pumps away at me.

He pushes down hard on my hip and his eyes lock onto mine.

"Good girl, Holly. Come for me. Prove why you should be on my nice list."

I whimper as the pressure builds deep inside me. We've done a lot of fucking over the last few days but there's something different this time, something deeper. Maybe because I'm restrained, maybe because of the way he's looking at me—like a meal—or maybe something else that I don't yet understand.

I come completely undone as he grinds away at my rear end. I cry out, my orgasm sweeping through my entire body. My legs shake, my skin tingles.

"Harder! Faster!" I shout.

He obliges, thrusting deeper, harder and faster and spinning my climax out into a long and rich tapestry of moans and expletives. I'm so lost in sensation that I'm barely aware when his thrusts become erratic and his eyes roll back in his head.. He comes with a throaty grunt and keeps pumping his hips, albeit more slowly and his pressure on my hip easing. I come down slowly and am still shaking when he withdraws and lays down in front of me. He unties my hands and I slowly untwist my body. Every part of me aches, in the best way. I grin stupidly at him.

"That was incredible," he says, his voice husky.

"It was. Can we do it again?" I chuckle and he laughs back.

"Give me half an hour."

I do. And we do.

CHAPTER SEVENTEEN

Light filters through my eyelids as I slip out of sleep. I could have sworn I just heard bells jingling, but maybe I dreamed them. Nicolas's warm body is pressed against my back. It's too light. It's either somehow lunch time, or...

My eyes flicker open to a room bathed in soft, white light. We left the curtains open last night and daylight spills in through the big window in front of me. Fluffy white clouds fill my view and falling from them are great big snowflakes.

"No way," I whisper.

Nicolas stirs. His arm tightens around me. But I ease myself out from under it and pad, naked, to the window. We're a thousand storeys up, no neighbours up here to peek inside. Still, I cross my arms over my chest and stare in wonder at the rare sight of a white Christmas in central London. A thin carpet of white covers everything, except for a few car tracks of charcoal grey in the roads below. The Thames remains its usual muddy brown, meandering past the apartment building. It's nowhere near cold enough to freeze the river, but still, I'll take what I can get.

"Morning," Nicolas murmurs behind me and I turn to face him, a grin lighting my face.

"It's snowing."

"Really?" He climbs out of bed and joins me at the window. He wraps his arms around me and kisses my neck. "Merry Christmas."

"Merry Christmas. What time is it?"

He cranes his neck towards the clock. "Nearly nine."

"Already? Shit. I have to go. My parents are expecting me."

"Us."

"Sorry?" I blink at him.

"They're expecting us. And not for another two hours. We've got time."

"No, wait. What?" I pull out of his arms and shake my head.

"While you were out with your friend last night I arranged everything. I'm coming with you."

He turns and heads for the bathroom. I gawk after him, unsure how I feel about this.

"Isn't it a bit soon for you to meet my family?" I say as I follow him and stand in the bathroom doorway. I watch him load his toothbrush with toothpaste.

"No." He radiates confidence and somehow I'm reassured. It is soon, but it's also Christmas and we've been through a hell of a lot. We've packed six extraordinary months of relationship into a few days. It's mad, but true.

Two hours later, we're climbing out of his car—no driver today, he has the day off—in Southgate and making our way up the snowy path to my parents' front door, arms full of bags. It's a semi-detached house with a drive and small front garden on a quiet street of nearly identical houses. It's painfully suburban and middle-class. But it's where I grew up, so it's still home. And yet, my stomach is knotted with nerves at bringing Nicolas to meet my parents.

The door opens before we reach it and my mum beams at us. She's wearing a nice dress and chunky cardigan and her blonde hair is neatly curled for the occasion.

"Hello!" She calls as we approach. "Merry Christmas!"

"Merry Christmas, Mum," I reply as we reach the door. She pulls me over the threshold and into a big hug. When she releases me I step aside and pull Nicolas forward. "This is Nicolas."

"Of course it is, lovely to meet you. Come on in."

"It's a pleasure to meet you, Mrs Harrington. This is for you," he says, holding out a potted poinsettia. She takes it with a gasp of delight and places it on the table by the door.

"Thank you, that's very kind." She hugs Nicolas too, and he grins at me over her head. He seems enormous in the narrow hallway of my childhood home. "I insist you call me Jenny," Mum says as she pulls out of his arms.

Movement at the other end of the hall catches my eye and I turn to see my Dad emerging from the kitchen, drying his hands on his apron.

"Hello, sweetheart," he says, smiling fondly at me. I toss my coat over the end of the bannister and practically run up to him for a hug.

"You alright, Dad?" I ask, still squeezing him.

"Fine, fine." He pats my back and I release him. He clears his throat and looks past me to our guest. "This young man must be Nick."

"Nicolas," I correct.

"Nick is fine," Nicolas says, smiling warmly as he hands Mum his coat.

I press my lips together and let them shake hands past me.

"Mr Harrington," Nicolas says politely.

"Robert." Dad gives a nod and releases Nicolas's hand. "Well, come in properly. How were the roads?" Dad asks as he leads us into the living room.

"It was really quiet," I reply. We step into the brightly lit room. The electric fire is glowing beside a five foot tree covered in brightly coloured lights and baubles. A small stack of presents sits beneath it, reflecting the lights in their shiny wrapping paper. "It looks lovely."

We get seated and Mum brings out a tray of glasses of sherry. Dad flits in and out of the kitchen while we engage in polite small talk and Mum bustles about. Nicolas rests his arm across the back of the sofa behind me and occasionally strokes my shoulder. A touch that grounds and reassures me.

Finally we all get settled around the tree and exchange gifts while Cliff Richard croons from the stereo. Mum and Dad laugh at the fact that they both bought each other socks. It's a running joke and Dad's gift tag even says "Oh no! Not socks again?!" There's the obligatory Terry's Chocolate Orange for each of us, including Nicolas, all from "Santa".

"How did he know I prefer the dark chocolate?" Nicolas asks with a wink as he opens his.

"He has his ways," Mum says, returning his wink.

I turn to Nicolas and pass him my gift. I watch him open it with a flutter of anticipation. His face lights up when he slides the tie out of its box.

"Do you like it?" I ask, though his face is all the answer I need.

"It's lovely, thank you." He leans forward and places a chaste kiss on my cheek. He turns and lifts a large gift bag with a big, gold bow on it. He passes it to me and my brow furrows with intrigue.

"What's this?"

"Open it and find out."

Inside the bag is a shoe box wrapped in gold paper. I lift it out and set the bag aside. Smiling cautiously, I unwrap the box and stop when I see the name printed across the top.

"No. You didn't."

"Well, I owed you a replacement for the pair you lost the other night."

"What did you lose?" Mum asks, peering over at us.

"But they weren't anything special. Just high street shoes. This is too much."

"What is?" Mum asks, growing impatient.

I glance her way and finally lift the lid on the shoebox. Inside is the most beautiful pair of shoes I've ever seen in my life. Clear PVC is studded with crystals. The heel is sparkling silver, a good ten centimetres and of course, the signature, bright red soles of Christian Louboutin.

"Ooh, they're pretty, Holly. Very you." Mum says, beaming.

"They are, but I can't accept them." I turn to Nicolas and wilt. He's smiling so sweetly.

"Your boyfriend has a lot of money. You're going to have to get used to accepting lavish gifts," he says, setting aside his usual humility. "Merry Christmas."

Boyfriend. Well, I guess that makes it official. If spending Christmas with my parents didn't already do that.

"Now then," Dad says, breaking the tension. "I'd better check on the turkey. Little help laying the table, pet?"

Mum takes one last, longing look at the shoes, then bustles off.

"I think Mum's jealous. These must have cost hundreds of pounds," I whisper, leaning close.

"Will you stop protesting and try them on?" He

smirks.

I could never have hoped to buy a pair of Louboutins in my life. Maybe I could enjoy the gift. I take off my shoes and socks and slip these on in their place. They're a perfect fit and goddammit, the irony strikes me.

"I feel like Cinderella," I say, half smiling, half aghast. Nicolas breaks into a hearty laugh, gets to his feet and hoists me up by my hands. I trot around the living room in my new glass slippers and enjoy playing princess.

We head into the dining room and help to lay the table. As I set the cutlery at each place setting, I smile, watching Nicolas chatting amiably with Mum. He's so at home in these fairly humble surroundings. He can move with ease between the boardroom, his penthouse, and my little life. I wonder if I'll ever do that.

The lunch is fabulous, as always. Dad is a great cook. The turkey is moist and seasoned to perfection, the parsnips, carrots and sprouts go down a treat. There's stuffing, roast potatoes, cranberry sauce and enormous Yorkshire puddings. We chase it all down with Christmas pudding covered in brandy sauce and retreat to the living room to let it settle. It's domestic bliss.

While Mum and Dad shed a tear over *The Snowman* on TV, Nicolas and I get stuck in to the washing up. I try not to giggle at the sight of him with his sleeves rolled up and his hands covered in bubbles.

"I don't think you should work for me any more."

"What?" I stare at him, frowning at this sudden

turn.

"I just mean," he says, keeping his voice low, "that I don't want you to be my subordinate. It doesn't feel right."

"Oh." He promised me I could keep my job. The sting is undeniable.

"I promised you'd have a job; you do—but not under me. There's a position for you with Halcyon." There's a slight tightening in his jaw.

"Your client?" I ask, slow, cautious. It feels as though a door that was left slightly ajar is beginning to open.

"Something like that. Your skills are just what they look for. You're bright, resourceful, you think on your feet. Your computer skills could be useful to them. I can set up a conversation, if you'd like."

"There's more to this than you're telling me," I say as I take a dish from the draining board and pat it dry.

"There is. And you need some field training."

"Field training?" I cock an eyebrow.

"You don't belong in spreadsheets any more," he says softly. "They can train you. Properly. For fieldwork, strategy... intelligence. You'd be brilliant."

I laugh, thinking he's kidding. But the laugh dies as I realise he's serious. "Intelligence?"

He cants his head and fixes me with a steady stare. "You aren't that naive, Holly. You got a first hand look at DUSK. Halcyon is their competition."

"Oh." I try to stamp out my shock. Because he's right, I did know that already, from my experiences.

And yet I hadn't quite put the pieces together. Maybe I hadn't wanted to. "Do you own Halcyon?"

"No. I work with them. They're a client. That's more or less true. I help to keep their funding clean. So we'd be working alongside each other. Equals." He smiles.

"Maybe I am done hiding behind a desk," I admit. The mention of clean funding lands deep in my chest. Money laundering. The impeccable Mr Sainz doesn't have such clean hands. It should scare me. But after everything that's happened, it feels inevitable. There's a weight to it, but I respect it, rather than fear it.

Dad wanders in from the living room with a glass of brandy in hand.

"You two look like you're plotting something."

"Just a little heist," Nicolas says with a wink. Dad laughs and a nervous squeak slips out of my mouth.

"Jolly good."

Once the washing up is done, we settle back on the sofa to watch another Christmas classic. I snuggle against Nicolas, my feet tucked up beside me, his arm resting around my shoulders and I realise this is what safety feels like. My new shoes stand under the tree, carefully placed, the twinkling lights glinting on the crystals.

"Merry Christmas," Nicolas murmurs.

"Best one yet, Santa." I reply.

THE BOOKBINDER'S FAREWELL

Every gift must one day be unwrapped... and every story, eventually, must close.

But endings are never truly endings, are they? Only thresholds. Doors to other rooms, other tales. The world is wider than you think—threads of intrigue and temptation stretching far beyond this page. You've tasted one secret tonight. Others wait, watching, waiting to be found.

Until then, keep your wits sharp, your heart guarded... and your desires unashamed.

I'll be waiting in the shadows, where every story begins.

THE HEAT DOESN'T HAVE TO END HERE

Want more of Holly & Nicolas?

Their fairytale isn't over yet.

Download the free bonus epilogue and step back into their world of glittering lights, stolen kisses, and Christmas magic on the edge of the world.

Because when love burns this bright, happily ever after is only the beginning.

Just one more sip...

You know you want it.

Download it here: https://BookHip.com/TVTGLVQ

Sign up to my newsletter for exclusive bonus content—including epilogues you won't find anywhere else.

It's free, filthy, and just a little bit forbidden.

See you between the pages, gorgeous.

Lacey xox